In college, Drew Menard was deep in the closet, too afraid to step out. That meant he missed his chance to follow up on the most amazing kiss of his life. He's always remembered who'd given it to him, though—Will Hanson. Drew had secretly watched Will at many a track meet and band performance. His biggest regret was never gathering enough courage to be himself and do something about it.

Almost seven years later, Drew no longer thinks of himself as in the closet, although he wouldn't consider himself out and proud, either. His friends know his orientation, even if his father doesn't. Why rock the boat when he has zero interest in anyone beyond one night?

All that changes when none other than Will walks through the door of the clinic where Drew works, and he discovers his desire for him hasn't waned one bit. While Will is accompanying a student in need of physical therapy, he can barely concentrate enough to do his job. Can Drew convince Will he's changed enough to give him a chance?

The Drum Major's Passion
Copyright © 2020 Charlie Richards
ISBN: 978-1-4874-3136-5
Cover art by Martine Jardin

Published by eXtasy Books Inc or
Devine Destinies, an imprint of eXtasy Books Inc

Look for us online at:
www.eXtasybooks.com or www.devinedestinies.com

The Drum Major's Passion
Carry Me: Book Eleven

By

Charlie Richards

DEDICATION

Christmas magic is silent. You don't hear it — you feel it, you know it, you believe it.
~Kevin Alan Milne

CHAPTER ONE

"Slow your reps," Drew Menard ordered levelly. "Focus on your form. This is a marathon, not a sprint."

Drew's client, Ned Lucre, glared straight ahead, but he obeyed. "I want my leg back to normal," he grumbled as a drop of sweat dripped down his temple. "Damn car accident."

Even having heard it all before, Drew nodded anyway. "I'm sorry that happened to you." He stated the platitude as he always did. Then Drew followed that up by reminding, "But according to your doctor, you'll make a full recovery as long as you put in the work." Seeing that Ned had begun speeding up his movements once more, he rested his palm on Ned's shoulder. "Ned, if you do the work wrong, you're going to re-injure yourself and set yourself back."

Resting his foot on the floor, Ned growled under his breath for an instant. He tipped his head back and heaved a deep sigh as he closed his eyes. "I know you're right," Ned grumbled. Refocusing on Drew, he nodded slowly. "Okay. So go slow with the bungee-band flexing."

"Exactly," Drew confirmed, straightening again. "We're strengthening your thigh muscles that were damaged by the breaking window glass."

As Ned's physical therapist, Drew knew the ins and outs of his injuries. Otherwise, he wouldn't have been able to guide him through his rehab.

For the next twenty minutes, Drew led Ned through a couple of other exercises to help the man strengthen the muscles that had been repaired by the doctor.

"Well done, Ned," Drew congratulated as a sweaty Ned moved his feet off the bicycle pedals to the floor. "Let's get you moved to the hot tub to soak your leg."

Ned nodded as he rubbed his sleeve over his forehead. "Yeah."

"Do you want your crutches, or should I wheel you in the chair?" Drew asked, knowing after the work-out, the man might need it.

Ned groaned as he pressed the back of his head into the cushion of the reclining bicycle. Turning his head, he squinted up at Drew. "Wheelchair."

Drew nodded, offering the man an understanding smile. "Probably a smart choice," he assured. "We'll get your leg rested so you'll be able to crutch on out of here." Drew finished teasing him with a rakish smile.

A low, rough chuckle escaped Ned. "Right."

Taking that, Drew headed to the wall and fetched the wheelchair. He returned to Ned's side. Bending, he slid his arm under his client's knees as the man slung his arm over Drew's shoulders.

As Drew moved the six-foot-two, well-muscled frame, he appreciated his own six-foot-four build. He'd played as a linebacker in college for several years, and he kept his powerful body in well-defined shape. Still, as Drew helped the guy move, Drew's muscles strained.

Plus, considering Ned was actually a damn fine specimen, Drew found himself struggling to control his prick.

Admitting to being gay had been a long road for Drew, but at least he no longer lied—to anyone—when they asked. As he straightened and stepped away from Ned, Drew was grateful his father would never think to ask that. He figured the man wouldn't understand. Drew knew his dad already didn't understand his job choice. His father thought Drew should have tried to pursue a future as a football player. That had never been Drew's dream, regardless of how good his dad thought he was.

Besides, not like I've ever met a man that would tempt me to enter a relationship.

One-night stands worked just fine for him.

Leaving Ned in the hot tub, Drew headed to the front desk. He spotted Jillian Parsons behind the counter and almost turned around. The woman worked part-time, splitting the receptionist position with another lady — Katie — and made a habit of asking him out at least once a week, and Drew was running out of excuses to give her.

It caused his working environment to be more than a little uncomfortable. He'd made a passing comment about it once to his boss — Rafe Litman — and the older man had chuckled. Then he'd made a comment about how great it would be to be young and desired.

Drew wondered what would happen if he told her he was feeling sexually harassed.

Just as Drew saw Jillian begin to turn in his direction, as if she had some *Drew Radar*, the bell over the lobby door dinged, drawing her attention. Relief filled him, but he figured that might not get him out of talking with her. At least with a client there, she would be a little professional.

Right? Hope so.

Closing the distance to the front desk, Drew watched Jillian sweep her gaze over whoever was entering. He took advantage and slipped Ned's file into her in-box. Then Drew turned and strode back down the hall again.

Drew had ten minutes before he needed to help Ned out of the hot tub. After that, he was done for the day.

"Hey, Drew," Jillian called. "Got a sec?"

Fighting back a cringed, Drew turned and pasted a smile on his lips. "Sure. What can I help you with?" he asked, keeping his voice level and professional as he watched Jillian hurry to his side.

"It looks like there was a mix-up in scheduling," Jillian stated, nibbling her bottom lip. "There's a young man here that was supposed to see Mister Mindrid today, but he's not in." Her brows were furrowed, yet still she lifted her hand to her chest, teasing her fingertips along the neckline of her shirt.

Drew figured she meant to be provocative, but it was completely lost on him.

"Mister Litman is already with a client," Jillian continued, her lips curving into a fake-concerned moue. "I know you're supposed to be off after Mister Lucre leaves, but do you have time for a consultation?"

Even if Drew had had plans, he would never leave a client hanging because someone—probably Jillian—had messed up the scheduling.

"Certainly," Drew replied. "I'll need to finish with Mister Lucre first. Can they wait?" Another thought struck him. "Are they okay with seeing a different physical therapist?"

Jillian glanced back toward the lobby, hesitating.

Drew clenched his jaw for a second before taking a calming breath. Except, his lungs were then filled with a cloying floral scent.

Ugh. Too much perfume again.

"I'll be back out shortly, Jillian," Drew told her, taking a step away. "If they're okay with a different therapist and are willing to wait, I'll pick them up then."

Then Drew pivoted and headed into the break room. He grabbed a bottle of water and swigged several gulps. After a glance at his watch, he saw he had a couple more minutes before returning to Ned.

Drew settled on a chair and stretched his legs out in front of him. Tipping his head, he rested it on the cushion. He focused on his breathing and relaxing the muscles of his neck and shoulders.

After a few minutes, Drew felt better. "Good thing tomorrow is Saturday," he muttered as he rose back to his feet. "Barbeque tonight at Jake's, and I know he'll let me crash there. Then a run with him in the morning."

Smiling, Drew headed back to Ned. "Feeling better?" he asked with a grin as he grabbed a towel.

"Getting better all the time," Ned replied, taking the towel.

To Drew's relief, his client sounded it, too.

After helping Ned from the hot tub and into the wheelchair, Drew took him to the changing room. "Don't forget to set up an appointment with Jillian for Monday," he reminded. After receiving confirmation from Ned, he left the man to it.

Drew returned to the front. Pausing at the opening, he swept his gaze around the area. His focus landed on the two waiting in the chairs there.

From the fact that the young man—a teenager around the age of fifteen—sported a large walking cast, Drew figured he was the client. He guessed the black-haired man with him would be his father. Then the adult turned his attention from the teenager and met his gaze.

Sucking in a shocked gasp, Drew peered into vibrant green eyes that had haunted his dreams for over six years.

"Will."

Will Hanson had given Drew his first kiss from a guy. While he indulged in one-night stands, he didn't kiss them—not anymore. Every time he'd kissed a trick, he'd been turned off. The memory of Will's soft lips pressed against his own slammed into Drew, causing his gut to clench and his mouth to tingle with sensory recall.

Rising to his feet, Will narrowed his eyes and swept his gaze over Drew. His expression said it all. He was trying to place him.

Damn. He doesn't remember me.

Drew sure as hell remembered Will. His thick black hair was longer than it had been in college, but he'd retained his lean runner's build. Back then, Will had worn black-rimmed glasses, but he wasn't wearing them now, making his green eyes seem even more vibrant.

Then Will's eyes widened a little, and his lips parted. "Drew?" he questioned softly. "Drew Menard?"

Unable to help himself, Drew grinned broadly. "Hey." He closed the distance between them, needing to get closer. "It's been years." Wanting to touch, Drew held out his hand. "How are you?"

Will hesitated an instant, then took Drew's hand. "Um, good. I'm good."

Drew felt Will's warm palm slide against his own, and he tightened his grip just a little. He wanted to hold onto the man. The urge to cradle Will's hand with his second one filled him, so he did it.

"Glad to hear it, Will. Really glad." Unable to help himself, Drew added, "We need to meet for coffee. Catch up."

Drew knew he needed to rein in his excitement at seeing his college crush again—and so out of the blue. His cock was already thickening in his slacks, and his pants weren't going to hide his excitement for long.

"Mister Hanson," a young masculine voice murmured.

Will pulled his hand from Drew's as he half-turned in the teenager's direction. "Pete, this is Mister Menard." With a glance Drew's way, he offered with a half-smile, "Sorry I didn't make the connection when the receptionist said you were available to talk to us." Before Drew could reassure the man, Will continued, "This is Pete Skarner."

Using his big head, Drew focused on Pete. "Hey, buddy." He gave the young man an encouraging smile. "Looks like you got yourself into a little trouble, huh?"

Pete scowled at Drew as he rolled his eyes. "Wasn't my fault."

"It never is," Drew countered, shoving his hands into his

pockets. If his hands were out of the way, maybe he could control his urge to touch Will again. "So, let's head back to my office to talk." Realizing he needed a bit more information, he turned and peered at Jillian. "Do you have Pete's file?"

Jillian nodded as she held up a file. "Right here." As she spoke, she rested one arm on her desk and leaned forward, using the move to push her boobs forward.

Drew kept his focus squarely on Jillian's face as he plucked the file from her fingers. "Thank you." Then he moved his attention back to Will and Pete. Drew saw Will helping Pete to his feet and offered, "I can get you a wheelchair if you need a break from those crutches."

Pete scowled at him. "I got it."

Great. Due to some error, I get to handle a belligerent teenager. Swell.

At least Pete's attitude caused Drew's arousal to ease.

Forcing himself to keep a professional smile on his face, Drew nodded. "Of course. Standard procedure to offer." He started walking. "If you'll both join me."

Drew led the way deeper into the clinic. When he passed Ned crutching his way to the front, he clapped him lightly on the upper arm. "See you Monday, Ned."

"Yep. Thanks, Drew."

Pointing his finger at Ned, Drew reminded him, "And don't forget what we discussed." That was all he could say in front of other clients.

Ned fixed him with a wry grin. "Yeah. Yeah."

Laughing lightly, Drew opened the door a few feet away. He led the way inside and indicated the chairs opposite his desk. Once they'd entered and headed that way, Drew closed the door and rounded his desk.

As Drew placed the file before him, he settled in his own chair. Glancing between Will and Pete, he realized he needed a little more information before he could get started. After all, he didn't know the relationship between the pair.

Can Will be involved in a confidential conversation?

"Uh, we didn't really know each other well in college," Drew began slowly, meeting Will's gaze. "And you have different last names." He opened the file and tapped it. "Will I find documentation in here telling me that I can discuss Pete's treatment in front of you, Will? Or do I need to ask you to leave?"

That was the last thing Drew wanted to do. He wanted to keep Will in view until he figured out a way to ask for the man's phone number. Still, he would do it for patient confidentiality reasons.

Please say you can stay.

CHAPTER TWO

Will Hanson still felt completely blown away—not only by the fact that he was sitting across from Drew Mcnard in a physical therapy office, but also by the way the man had greeted him . . . as if they were old friends.

Why would he do that?

They hadn't spoken or even been within fifty feet of each other since Will had kissed Drew. He still remembered the impulsive moment as if it were yesterday instead of almost seven years before.

In college, Will had been a year ahead of Drew. He would have been considered a band geek if he hadn't also had a lean runner's build and had been on the track team. Will had excelled at both the sprinting events and the middle distance races—easily able to pace himself up to thirty-two-hundred meters at speed.

Will had enjoyed practicing at night, running on the track after the football team had finished their practice. Most of the time, he managed to make certain he arrived after all the players had left the locker room. As an openly gay student who was part of the gay pride alliance, Will was aware he could be a target for testosterone-fueled jocks.

Occasionally, Will arrived too early—or some of the guys took longer than normal in the locker room—and they'd jeered him as he'd run. As with any group of bullies, Will had ignored them. Fortunately, with his head focused on the burn of his muscles and the movement of his limbs, Will had always found it easy to lose himself in running.

One evening, one of the jocks had decided he'd had enough with being ignored. He'd stepped into Will's path. Will's memories took him as he recalled what happened next.

Will barely managed to avoid ramming into the jock's muscular, taller frame. Instead, Will clipped him on the arm as he'd swerved.

"Don't you touch me, faggot," the jock roared, shoving Will, even though it had been his own fault. "I don't want your taint."

Will planned to turn and keep running. Hell, he could outdistance the guy and the pair flanking him on his worst day. Before he could move, the jock grabbed his upper arm.

So much for not touching him.

"You don't get to ignore me," the jock snarled. "I told you yesterday that I didn't wanna see you around here no more."

Will so wanted to correct the jock's speech patterns, but he figured that would just make it worse. "I'm part of the track team," he stated, keeping his voice as level as possible. "I have permission to use the track."

In fact, as long as no actual coach-led training was going on, anyone could use the track whenever they wanted.

"I don't give a shit," the jock replied belligerently. "I say your fag ass don't come 'round here no more, so you do as I say." Then he released Will and cracked his knuckles. "Or else."

The two guys flanking the asshole chuckled cruelly.

Will barely resisted rolling his eyes. It seemed he would have to report these guys to his coach after all. He'd been hoping to avoid dragging administration into it, but the college did have a zero-bullying policy in place, so he might as well take advantage of it.

Huh. Wonder if it'll work.

Just as Will opened his mouth to warn the jock one last time, a deep voice caught everyone's attention.

"Leave him alone, Aaron," the interloper ordered, a low growl filling his tone.

The sexy voice went straight to Will's groin, causing his blood to heat.

Well, damn!

"You sidin' with this homo, Drew?" one of the other jocks asked, clearly surprised. "What the hell, man?"

The man—Drew—crossed his arms over his massive torso, accentuating his bulging biceps. "I'm not siding with anyone but the right to work out in peace, Kyle," Drew stated, frowning as he glanced between the trio. The man had an inch or more on the others, depending on the jock. "This guy isn't doin' anything but training. That's his right. How'd you like it if some asshole came into the weight room and ordered you to leave while you were pumping iron?"

The ringleader—Aaron—snorted as he leveled a narrow-eyed glare at Drew. "No one would do that, since I ain't a disgusting homo faggot."

Drew rolled his eyes. "Maybe they would decide to do it because you're a bully who needs a taste of his own medicine." Before Aaron could respond, Drew held up his phone. "Besides, if you don't stop harassing Will, I'll give this video to coach. You wanna get benched a coupla games?"

Aaron scoffed, but the other guys exchanged uneasy glances. "Coach wouldn't bench me."

"Zero tolerance, remember?" Drew stated, revealing he was aware of the policy, too. "Even if he didn't want to, he'd have to." Rolling one boulder of a shoulder in a half-shrug, Drew smirked. "But he'd *want* to. Coach Harrison never let you pick on Jake. Why would he let you bully some other gay dude?"

"You bein' tainted by your fag roommate, Drew?" Aaron taunted, stalking toward him. "You a butt-muncher now? Are ya bonin' that loser cuz ya can't get no pussy?"

Narrowing his dark eyes, Drew shook his head. "God, do

you even listen to yourself? Why are you thinkin' of me and Jake's sex lives?" Then his expression turned sad as he shook his head. "I'm really sorry, Aaron. Even though me and Jake ain't bangin, I can't really put in a good word for ya with my roommate. You're just not Jake's type."

To Will's amusement, Aaron's pale face flushed red as he took a step backward as if struck. "I don't want anythin' to do with that homo. I'm so fuckin' glad he's off the team." His voice lowered as he grumbled, "Fags shouldn't play ball."

"He was a better runningback than Tom, here," Drew claimed, flicking his hand toward the shorter of the black men who'd been flanking Aaron. "No offense, man."

Tom shrugged. "None taken."

Aaron scowled at Tom. "How can you say that?" he barked. "Of course, you're better than that homo."

Wincing for an instant, Tom muttered, "Jake was good, A. I know you don't want to admit that, but it's true." He shook his head. "If he hadn't quit, I wouldn't be seein' nearly as much game time as I am now."

"Come on, A," the final guy encouraged. "This ain't worth it, and I got shit to do."

Will watched Aaron mentally debate with himself — emotions flitting across his features. It was obvious the jock didn't understand how he'd lost the support of his buddies.

"Whatever," Aaron snarled. After casting a disgusted look at Drew, he glanced over his shoulder at Will. "Watch your back, faggot, and stay off my track."

Drew stood nearby, waiting and watching with Will as the trio disappeared into the night.

Clearing his throat, Drew rubbed the back of his neck as he turned his focus on Will. "Um, you should probably report Aaron," he muttered. "I'm not sure he's gonna let this drop, and he'll probably try something underhanded next time." With a shake of his head, Drew added, "He's a dick like that."

Will nodded. "If I need that video, can I get it from you?" Closing the distance between them, he held out his hand. "Drew, is it? I assume you're on the football team, too?"

Drew hesitated just an instant as he nodded before taking his hand.

At first, Will thought it was because Drew wasn't certain about touching a gay guy. Then he recalled how he was the roommate of one, and they had sounded as if they had a good rapport. Except, when Drew's huge, calloused palm slid into Will's own and he saw the way the much larger man sucked in a harsh breath as his nostrils flared, the truth hit Will.

He's attracted to me, too. This man is gay? Or at least bi?

Will squeezed lightly while stepping even closer. When Drew didn't pull away or attempt to free his hand, Will offered him a shy smile and peered at him from beneath his lashes. It was a little difficult through his glasses, but Will had learned how to make it work.

"I appreciate the warning, too," Will murmured, making his tone a little husky. He didn't miss the way Drew's eyes dilated and how his breathing hitched. "That was a nice thing you did."

"I-I was, um—" Drew paused and cleared his throat. After his tongue flicked out, wetting his lower lip, he gruffly mumbled, "H-Happy to help."

With the way Drew was staring at him, Will felt his blood flow south. He couldn't remember the last time a guy had looked at him with so much appreciation. While Will had never been one to admire jocks—he knew that could be a recipe for getting his ass kicked—he couldn't help but admire Drew's big, broad, thickly muscled frame.

He's gotta be a lineman or something.

"I'd like to thank you properly," Will told Drew, easing even more into the much larger man's personal space. "Can I?"

Drew stared down their several inches in height difference

for a few seconds. While a look of uncertainty filled his features, there was desire there, too. "Uh, sure?" he whispered.

Taking a chance, Will rested his free hand on Drew's chest. He felt the man's massive torso twitch under his touch, but Drew didn't move away. Will leaned into the man and lifted onto his toes, allowing him to bring their faces closer together.

When Drew still didn't move away from him, Will felt his own blood speed up in his veins. Anticipation filled him. After another second of hesitation, Will pressed his lips to Drew's.

Drew reacted instantly, and Will almost reared back, thinking he'd made a horrible miscalculation. Except, he couldn't move . . . because Drew had wrapped his free arm around Will's waist. In the same instant, he yanked his other hand free of Will's and sank it into Will's hair.

With a tug at Will's hair and a nip on his lower lip, Drew forced his head to the side and his mouth to part. The big jock thrust in his tongue, delving into Will. He plundered and conquered, controlling the kiss while mapping his cavity.

Will gripped Drew's shirt, hanging on for the ride — and what a ride it was.

By the time Drew broke the kiss, Will's lips tingled, his lungs burned, and his blood pounded in his veins. It took every bit of self-control he possessed to keep from rubbing his aching erection against Drew's thick thigh. Panting, he forced his eyelids open and stared up at the guy who'd just given him the best kiss of his life.

Drew's lips gleamed in the lights illuminating the track. His eyes were wide, and his cheeks were flushed. The big body pressed against Will's own shuddered against him.

Then Will took in Drew's expression — a look that could only be called shell-shocked.

"Drew?" Will murmured, hoping to snap the man out of it.

Will watched Drew blink once, twice, and relief began to

14

fill him.

Except, then Drew focused on Will and gasped. "Oh, shit," he hissed as he jumped away from him.

Stumbling from the sudden loss of Drew's body for support, by the time Will caught his balance, Drew was gone. Sighing, he shook his head. That certainly hadn't turned out as he'd hoped.

"What did I really expect?" Will muttered as he turned toward a different exit to the track, one that would leave him closer to his dorm.

There was no way he would be able to keep running with the boner he sported.

Instead, Will returned to his dorm and —

"Will can stay." Pete's voice yanked Will out of his memory. "There's a note in there about him being allowed to know my medical history."

"Glad to hear it," Drew replied, flashing a wide grin. "Then let's get started."

Will did his best to focus on the situation — helping the young man he worked with through the *Big Brother* program get the physical therapy he needed.

CHAPTER THREE

"You'll never guess who came into my office today." Drew couldn't keep the smile off his face or the eagerness from his voice.

His buddy, Jake Gateman—formerly Jake Lewis—arched one brow as he relaxed against his husband's side on the sofa. "Why don't you tell me who walked into your office today," he stated with a smirk. Then he sobered. "Unless it'd break patient confidentiality or something."

Jake's husband, Devon, chuckled as he squeezed his arm tighter around his man's shoulders. "If that was the case, surely Drew wouldn't have brought it up."

"Oh, right." Jake nodded, beaming at his husband. "That makes sense." Then they leaned close and shared a short kiss.

Drew stared off to the left as he took a swig of his beer. His stomach was happily full of delicious steak that Jake had grilled earlier. Even then, he leaned forward and snagged a tortilla chip, swiped it through the bowl full of guacamole, and popped it into his mouth.

Fortunately, by the time he'd chewed and swallowed, his friends had finished their brief, sickenly sweet lip-lock.

Jake offered him a wry smile. "Um, so you were saying?"

With a grin of his own, Drew announced, "Will Hanson."

Devon's brows drew together, betraying his confusion. Even Jake appeared uncertain. Cocking his head, his buddy's expression turned a little vacant.

"I know that name," Jake murmured softly. A few seconds later, his eyes widened, and he snapped his attention back to

Drew. "Will Hanson as in *the best kiss of your life* Will Hanson?"

Drew felt his cheeks heat, but he nodded anyway.

"Holy shit!" Jake cried. "It's been . . . what? Five years since you've seen him? Six?"

"Closer to seven," Drew admitted.

"Since when does Drew kiss?" Devon asked absently, continuing to express his confusion.

Chuckling, Drew rolled his eyes. He understood where Devon's question was coming from. Even though there was an age gap between Jake and Devon—Devon was over a decade Jake's senior—the man had taken Jake to a few clubs, just to see if it was something Jake would enjoy.

It hadn't been.

Still, Drew and a few others in their circle of friends had joined them, and it was well-known that Drew didn't kiss pick-ups. He'd had a few prospective one-night stands walk away from him because of it. Remembering there were always more fish in the sea, he'd never minded.

"Come on, dude," Carmen piped up from his position on another sofa. Devon's younger brother had his arm slung around his partner's shoulders—Tyler—and played with the man's hair. "Answer the question. You don't kiss."

Jake waved his hand, getting everyone's attention as he swallowed the sip of red wine he'd taken after his outburst. "Why do you think Drew doesn't kiss?" he stated, snickering. "No one could compare to Will's liplock, so he stopped trying." With a wink, Jake finished, "It rocked his world, knocked his socks off, and shut his mind down so badly he didn't remember running back to his dorm in a haze of panicked pleasure."

Drew glared at Jake, growling under his breath. "Asshole. That was supposed to be in the best friend secrecy vault." His cheeks felt on fire as he recalled how he'd returned to his dorm in a panic after kissing Will that fateful night. "But, yeah. He sorta ruined me for anyone else."

After admitting that, Drew swigged down the rest of his brew.

"Oh, wow," Tyler murmured, leaning forward. "So, what happened after that?" When Drew just looked at him vacantly, the flamboyant man flapped his hand. "You know, after you settled down in the dorm? Did you see him again?" Waggling his brows, Tyler asked, "Enjoy some sweaty nights of hot sex? How'd you break up?"

"Uhhhh." Drew grimaced, feeling self-conscious. Still, these were his friends. Rubbing the back of his neck, Drew admitted, "I stayed away from him. I was still playing football, and I worried . . . um—" Drew sighed and grimaced at the ceiling.

To Drew's relief, Jake picked up his tale. "Drew wasn't ready to come out of the closet, and Will was a year ahead of him," he explained to their friends. "By the time Drew was ready to start experimenting at the end of his fourth year, Will had graduated and gone who knows where."

"I suppose I could have tracked him down," Drew admitted. "But what the hell would I say?" Taking the fresh beer from Lester—a guy he and Jake had befriended in college when they'd spotted him being bullied—Drew muttered his thanks. Popping off the cap, Drew sarcastically answered his own question, "Hey, remember me? I'm the guy who ran away after we kissed that one time almost two years ago. I'm ready now. How about a date?"

Devon chuckled softly as he shook his head. "Well, I wouldn't use those *exact* words, but maybe some variation?"

Sitting on the far end of the sofa from Jake and Devon, Rory—another friend from college—asked speculatively, "Did Will remember you?"

Drew immediately began to nod. Then he paused a second

before nodding once more. "Yeah." He rubbed a hand over his cheeks, trying to get the circulation to remove his blush. "It took him a minute, but yeah, he remembered me."

"And is he single?" Rory continued.

"Uhhhhhh—" Drew snapped his mouth shut, then admitted, "I don't know."

Sighing, Jake asked, "Did you at least get his phone number?" Then he frowned. "If he's not a client, what was he doing there?" Then Jake groaned. "Please don't tell me he was escorting his husband."

Drew swiftly shook his head. "No. No, of course not. You all know I'd never poach."

His buddies had all had experiences with cheating exes — except for Jake and Devon, but since Devon's mother had been a cheating whore that had ended up leaving his father with the raising of five boys, it amounted to the same thing.

Scoffing, Carmen assured, "We know, man. Relax." He flashed an encouraging smile Drew's way. "So, the phone number?"

Nodding, Drew told them, "Yeah, I got his number." Clearing his throat, he admitted, "I might have swiped it from the file of the young man he'd been escorting." When he saw Devon frown at him — the older man owned a chiropractic practice and probably figured it was a breach of etiquette, but Drew didn't care. "Come on, Dev. This is my chance. Besides, I'd already asked him to meet up for coffee to catch up, and he'd said yes."

Wait. Did he say yes?

Drew couldn't remember, but he didn't care, either.

Devon snorted and smirked.

Awesome. I'm forgiven.

"So, back to the *is he single* question," Rory reminded.

"Uhhhh . . ." Drew didn't know how to answer that. Just thinking that Will was already in a relationship caused his gut to churn. Finally, he had to admit, "I don't know." When his friends exchanged concerned glances, Drew rolled his eyes. "Come on. Not like I could ask him on a date in front of the client he was with."

"Yeah, totally," Jake stated, jumping to his defense. "Of course not. So we gotta find out." Leaning forward, he grabbed the wine bottle off the coffee table and refilled his stemware.

"How are we gonna do that?" Lester asked doubtfully.

"How about a picture?" Jake asked, offering the bottle to Rory, who took it and topped off his own glass before setting aside the bottle. "Did you manage to snag a pic of him to show us?"

Drew felt his face heat as he shifted uncomfortably in his seat. "Yeah," he muttered before taking a swig of his beer in the hopes of his cheeks cooling down.

Gods, this is so embarrassing. This is why I don't date. Too fucking hard.

"Oh, let's see him," Tyler urged, making a beckoning motion with one upturned hand.

Heaving a deep sigh, Drew knew he couldn't get out of it. He pulled his phone out of his pocket and woke the device. After a few taps on his phone, Will's lean frame filled the screen.

Drew had snapped the picture when Will had stopped at Jillian's desk to schedule Pete's appointment. The shot had a perfect view of his profile. His lean frame, encased in nice jeans and a polo shirt, were almost silhouetted by the black, thigh-length winter coat he had draped over his far arm.

Gorgeous.

"Oh, damn. Look at that smile," Rory teased, chuckling. "Still smitten with the one that got away."

Glaring, Drew grumbled, "Why do I call you my friend?" He passed his phone to Tyler.

Rory just laughed.

"Hmmm . . . Will is pretty fine," Tyler commented, earning

him a growl from Carmen. Giving his boyfriend an innocent look, Tyler quickly added, "Not as fine as you, of course, my love."

"Better," Carmen grumbled. Then he winked and looked at the phone. "Will does have a hot schoolteacher vibe going for him, though."

"Hand it over," Jake demanded, holding out his hand. "My turn."

Tyler dutifully handed it over.

While Drew took a sip of his beer, he eyed his buddy who was staring at his phone.

Jake hummed. "Definitely hotter than in college," he commented while swiping over the phone's surface. "Is that the only picture you took?" As Jake asked that, he began tapping at the surface.

Is Jake looking for more photos of him?

Drew frowned. "Yeah. That's the only one." When he saw Jake nod in an almost absent manner while continuing to tap his phone, Drew leaned forward. "Hey. What are you doing?"

With the way Devon's brows were creeping up his forehead, a niggle of concern filled Drew. Especially when Jake didn't respond.

Rising to his feet, Drew demanded, "Jake? Give me my phone."

"No," Jake snapped back. With a quick glance up, he ordered, "Don't let him near, Ror."

Rory immediately jumped to his feet, placing his wine glass on the end table where he'd set the bottle earlier. "Stay there," his friend ordered.

Drew growled, intending to go around him. While Rory was the same height as him — six-foot-four — his build was all wiry muscle. He also took martial arts, which he easily used to deflect Drew's attempts to get around him and to his phone.

The others quickly jumped from their seats and backed

away, giving them both space. Devon even steered Jake, who was still completely focused on Drew's phone, away from the living space with him.

"What the fuck are you doing?" Drew roared, hearing his phone ding, which indicated an incoming text.

Jake grinned widely. "Helping you," he finally told him, once more tapping on Drew's phone.

"Damn it, Jake." Drew tried to duck around Rory, who grabbed his arm and used his momentum to swing him back the other way. "Give it to me!"

"I will not," Jake told him, still tapping. "I'm helping you set up a meeting with Will."

Upon hearing that, Drew froze. "What?" His heart skipped a beat in his chest. "What have you done?"

Continuing to grin, Jake stated, "Well, first I texted, *Seeing you again was like a sun brightening my dismal life. Your sparkling emerald eyes made my breath catch, and your wide smile made my heart thud in my chest. Please tell me there's a chance I can show you how much you could mean to me.*"

Drew gaped, actually able to feel the blood drain from his face. "What?" he whispered, barely managing to choke out the word.

How could my friend do this to me?

Jake rolled his eyes and finally held out the phone to him. "Here."

With a shaking hand, Drew took it. Rory read over his shoulder, but with his focus on the screen, he couldn't move to push him away.

The message was nothing like what Jake had said.

Hi, Will. This is Drew. Since you said you wouldn't mind having coffee with me to catch up, I hope you don't mind me contacting you. Do you have any free time this weekend?

To Drew's surprise, Will's reply had been almost immediate.

Hi, Drew. Sure. I can meet you for coffee to catch up. How about

Sunday at ten?

Jake's response on his phone read — *That would be fine. Do you know Lady Jay's Coffee Shop on Fourth and Main?*

Oh, yeah. That place has awesome cinnamon rolls.

It does! Coffee and cinnamon rolls at ten on Sunday. See you then.

See you.

When Drew lifted his focus back to Jake, who had his arms crossed over his chest and a smug smile on his face, he mumbled, "Holy shit."

His friends laughed, but at least they started offering suggestions about what to talk about.

CHAPTER FOUR

*I*s *this a date? It feels like a date. No, he didn't say it was a date. This is just a couple of college buddies catching up, right? Except, we weren't buddies in college. But he didn't call it a date, either.*

Will's thoughts went round and round as he walked toward the coffee shop. He didn't really want to analyze how he'd felt when he'd read the text from the unknown number. Except, Will didn't make it a habit of lying to himself.

Excitement. Pulse-pounding excitement.

Why?

Sadly, Will knew the answer to that, too. It had been quite a while since he'd been pursued by anyone. Over the last few years, he'd been so focused on his career that he hadn't made time to date.

Except, this isn't a date, right?

God, I don't know!

After spotting Drew sitting at a table through the coffee shop window, Will forced back his confused mental ramblings. He paused at the door and took a deep, steadying breath. Then Will grabbed the handle and pulled open the door.

Will strode inside, the fragrance of sweets and coffee wrapping around his senses. Inhaling deeply as his mouth watered, he turned and met Drew's gaze. After dipping his chin in a nod, Will headed to the counter.

There was only one person before him, so the wait wasn't long. He requested a double caramel macchiato and a cinnamon roll. Mentally, he ordered himself to spend an extra fifteen minutes on the treadmill when he worked out that evening.

December in Oregon could have unpredictable weather, and it was supposed to storm that evening. He'd converted his basement into a home gym years before. As much as he loved running, he had no desire to do it while drenched if he didn't have to.

Taking his coffee and pastry, Will headed toward the table where his coffee companion rose from his seat. "Hi, Drew," he greeted. After placing his purchases on the table, Will held out his hand. "Good to see you again."

Drew grinned broadly, placing his hand in Will's. Just like the first time, the big man squeezed lightly and didn't release him right away.

"It's good to see you again, Will," Drew told him. "Thanks for agreeing to meet with me."

"Sure," Will replied, uncertain what else to stay. He cleared his throat and tugged gently on his hand.

A hint of pink filled Drew's cheeks as he released him and cleared his throat. "Oh. I already got us both a cinnamon roll." He indicated the two pastries already on the table as he took his seat. "But I didn't know what kind of coffee you'd want."

Flattered, Will smiled as a butterfly fluttered in his gut. "Oh, wow. Thanks." Easing onto his seat, he offered, "How about I take that home, and before we leave, I'll grab whatever pastry you want for you to take home."

Drew's brows shot up in obvious surprise. A second later, a pleased smile curved his thick lips. "Hey, thanks." He picked up one of the forks on the table and began pulling off the outer ring of the icing-topped pastry. "So, I have a confession to make."

Grabbing his own fork, Will cocked his head. "Um, okay." He started to cut into his cinnamon roll even as he smirked.

"That's never an ominous way to start a coffee date." Realizing what he'd said, he shifted in his seat. "Uh, not that I expected this to be a date," he said, trying to back-track. "Because I'd never want to presume. I only mean—"

"I want it to be a date," Drew cut in, stopping his yammering. "I really do." Stabbing the bit of cinnamon roll he'd unfurled, he admitted, "But I wasn't the one who texted you."

"Huh?" Will frowned. Before popping his bite of food into his mouth, he asked, "Then who did, since you're obviously here?"

Drew's cheeks darkened. "I was telling my buddies about running into you, and—" He paused and heaved a sigh while grimacing. "Well, Jake knew I wouldn't have the balls to actually message you, even though I wanted to, so he swiped my phone. He's the one who actually opened contact."

Unable to help himself, Will chuckled softly. "Opened contact. Interesting way to put it." Seeing the rosy hue of embarrassment darken Drew's cheeks, he sobered. "Well, I'm glad he did. It's been a long time since I've been on a date." Will realized there was something important he needed to know. "Since you want this to be a date, should I assume that you're out as gay?" After a second of hesitation, he added, "Or bi?"

Lifting his hand in a so-so gesture, Drew admitted, "Gay, yes. I'm not in the closet anymore, but—"

When Drew hesitated, Will pressed, "But?" With his coffee companion continuing to pause, he knew he needed to press the issue just a little. "Look, Drew. You're a good-looking guy, and I think you realized I was attracted to you in college." *Duh. I kissed him, after all.* "But I refuse to be anyone's dirty little secret. Been there, done that, got the t-shirt," he quipped, trying to soften his strident words. "If you're not comfortable with admitting you're on a date with me, then maybe it would be best if we just stayed friends."

"I'm out to my friends," Drew told him, lifting his hand to

stall Will's denials. "And I'm sorry someone asked that of you." Then Drew reached over and traced his fingertips over Will's hand where it rested on the table, although he didn't actually take his hand. "I've never told my dad I'm gay, but if I was ever serious about anyone, I would."

"Really?" Will couldn't keep the surprise from his tone.

Drew nodded. "Really."

Will didn't know if he believed Drew. He'd heard those words before. However, the fact that he was out to his friends certainly settled some of his reserves. After all, Drew had told him one of his buddies—a guy named Jake—had helped him set up the coffee date.

Wait. I'm totally getting ahead of myself.

"Okay, soooo . . . where do we go from here?" Will asked, only after saying the words realizing how awkward they sounded. Will knew it was his turn to blush by the warming of his neck. "Um, sorry. Been a while since I dated." He did his best to cover his *faux pa* by taking a sip of his drink.

Yeah, I've already said that, too. Dang it!

Chuckling, Drew shrugged. "And I've *never* dated." Then he waggled his eyebrows. "But I hear you're supposed to share life experiences, likes and dislikes, and shit like that."

Will snorted as he nodded. "Got it." Stabbing his fork into his cinnamon roll for another bite, he asked, "So, how long have you worked at that clinic as a physical therapist?"

"I did my apprentice work there and was really fortunate to get hired on right out of college," Drew told him, sporting an expression of relief. "It helped that my mentor really liked my style. Oh, that's Mister Mindrid, by the way. He was the one Pete was actually supposed to see."

Will nodded. "What was up with the scheduling change, if you don't mind my asking."

"Jillian can be a little scatterbrained sometimes," Drew told him with a grimace. "Especially if she's distracted by flirting with someone."

"You mean by flirting with you?" Will asked pointedly, unable to help himself. Seeing Drew wince, he snorted. "Yeah, I noticed. Does she not know?" Another thought entered his mind. "Or is she one of those women who thinks if you get together with *the right girl*" —he lifted the hand not holding his fork and made air quotes—"suddenly you won't be gay anymore?"

Drew shook his head. "Naw, she doesn't know."

That brought Will up short. "Are you not out at work?" When Drew had said his friends knew and he was no longer in the closet, he'd made assumptions.

I should know better than to do that.

"The other physical therapists know, and they don't care," Drew answered. "I told them when they offered me the job. I didn't want it to cause problems later on."

"Ah, okay."

That was good.

"What about you?" Drew asked, bring his coffee to his lips. "What are you up to these days?"

"I'm a music instructor and assistant band director at Colina High School," Will told him. "I'm also the drum major for the marching band."

Drew nodded, his brows furrowing. "Uh, so what does a drum major do?"

Swallowing his bite of food quickly, Will thought about how to explain. "I essentially lead the band, even though I don't play an instrument in it. It consists of leading them while marching, controlling how fast to march and play the music, deciding what to play, as well as when to take breaks or start playing again."

With parted lips, Drew eyed him up and down. "Wow," he murmured. "Sounds complicated."

Will shrugged. "I suppose." It had taken him almost a decade to get to his level. "Now it's pretty second nature to me."

Giving Drew a disarming grin and willing to push the attention to something else, Will pointed out, "You probably put in just as much work to get your position. I remember you played football in college."

Drew's lips curved into a fond smile as he appeared to be mentally recalling his past. "Yeah."

"I'd think going from football to physical therapy was a big change," Will pointed out before sipping his coffee. "Why'd you do it? Didn't want to go professional?"

Rolling one massive shoulder in a half-shrug, Drew told him, "My dad wanted me to go professional." He scoffed and shook his head. "He still doesn't understand why I quit, but once I come out to him, he will." Frowning, Drew muttered, "Or he'll never talk to me again."

"This is our first date, Drew," Will stated solemnly. "Shouldn't you wait until we discover if we're really into each other first?" He didn't want the handsome man putting his life into upheaval if after a week, they discovered they weren't compatible. "We should really get to know each other before you make that kind of decision."

Drew's smile appeared almost chagrined. "Will, I never forgot you. Not in all these years." Snorting softly, he muttered, "Did you know I used that single kiss as a benchmark for every other man's, and they all fell short?" Sighing deeply, Drew admitted, "After the first couple of years, I stopped kissin' altogether. It always left me feeling . . . disappointed."

Will gasped softly. His heart thudded in his chest. He felt a mixture of shock and pride. "Wow," he finally managed when he realized Drew stared at him expectantly. "Th- That's . . . amazing."

Clearing his throat, Drew shifted in his seat. "Anyway, to answer your question," he began, obviously trying to change the subject. "I was injured in my junior year. Knocked me out for the season. I was impressed with every aspect of physical therapy and sports medicine and asked my therapist a million questions." Shaking his head, Drew smiled wryly at him. "No way did I wanna go through years and years of medical school to be in the sports medicine field, but the therapy aspect really drew me. I switched majors my senior year, much to my dad's disappointment."

"The whole professional football thing, huh?" Will confirmed.

Drew nodded. "He thought I was good enough, but I didn't want to devote my life to a sport where I would have to hide who I am." Grimacing, he added, "Of course, I didn't tell him that. He still can't figure out why I'm such good friends with Jake, who's openly gay and married to his husband, Devon." Drew's cheeks began to pinken. "He's made a comment or two about how people could get the wrong idea, so maybe I should find a nice girl to settle down with."

Will grimaced. "Think you coming out is going to throw him for a loop? Or be pissed?" He'd heard of so many different reactions from family.

"Not sure," Drew admitted. "But I'll deal with it." Then he pushed away his now-empty plate and wrapped both hands around his paper cup. "What about your family? How'd yours take it?"

"It's just me and my mom," Will told him, thinking of his mother, who still attended pride parades with him. "I came out to her when I was thirteen."

Drew gaped. "Thirteen?"

Will chuckled at his expression. "Yep, when I told her I wanted to marry Dwayne Johnson."

To Will's pleasure, Drew tipped his head back and laughed.

CHAPTER FIVE

"So, how did your date go?"

Drew whipped around, surprised to see a smirk on Mister Alex Mindrid's face. The man was usually so focused on work that his smiles were always professional. He also rarely questioned anyone's personal life.

"Uh, great," Drew replied automatically. Narrowing his eyes, he quickly asked, "How'd you know I had a date?"

Alex's smirk turned into a grin. "No one smiles that big on a Monday morning unless they've had a fantastic weekend." He even waggled his eyebrows playfully. "Ergot, a date."

Laughing, Drew nodded. "Yeah. I guess that's true."

Sobering, Alex stated, "Please tell me you didn't finally give in and take Jillian on a date."

Drew rolled his eyes as he shook his head. "Of course not. I'm gay, remember?"

Alex shrugged. "Sometimes people do weird stuff to get someone off their back. Maybe you're grinning so widely because you took her out and gave her the worst date in history." He chuckled at his own idea. "That way, she'll never angle for another date from you again."

Snorting, Drew rested his hand on his hip. "Damn. Wish I would've thought of that." He scoffed as he added, "Of course, probably not the best way to handle it since it would make office life awkward."

"True." Tucking his clipboard under his arm, Alex asked, "So, who was the lucky guy?"

"His name is Will, and he's going to be escorting the client

I'm seeing in fifteen minutes, if you want to meet him." Drew's heart began to race. He'd never mixed business with pleasure before, and he wondered if this was crossing a line. "Uh, but Will isn't my client. He's the driver."

"Ah, yes." Alex nodded. "Rafe told me about the scheduling mix-up. Thank you for stepping in." A scowl suddenly tugged at his lips as he told him, "This isn't the first mix-up like this, but I sure hope it'll be the last."

"Last?" Drew couldn't help but pry. "What's that mean?"

Alex lowered his voice. "You didn't hear this from me, but Jillian received a warning for it." After a glance toward the breakroom door, confirming that it was closed, he continued, "If she does it again, she's out."

"Damn," Drew murmured. While he didn't wish ill on anyone, he wondered if that might not be for the best. "I, uh, I don't know what to hope for in this case. Training someone new would suck, after all."

Snorting, Alex told him, "Nice save."

Drew winked. "Thanks." His phone's ring saved him from having to come up with some other platitude. He pulled the device from his belt. "Speak of the devil." Taking in Alex's grin, Drew answered. "Hello, Jillian."

"Hey, Drew," she greeted in a chipper voice. "Your four o'clock is here. Should I tell him you'll be out soon?"

"Yes, tell them I'll be right out," Drew instructed. "Thank you." Then he hung up without waiting for a response. "See you later, Mister Mindrid."

Even as the man nodded, he called, "When are you going to call me Alex?"

Drew grinned as he headed toward the exit. "Maybe when I've officially been part of this practice for more than a couple of years," he told him.

Alex shook his head, but there was a smile on his face.

Good enough.

Striding down the hallway, Drew felt his heart race and his

palms sweat. He rubbed them on his jeans as he breathed deeply, trying to get himself under control. Reminding himself that he was at his place of work, he knew he needed to remain professional.

"Hey, Drew," Jillian called as soon as she spotted him. She held up a file, but when Drew reached for it, she pulled it away playfully. "Your legs look fantastic in those jeans. Are they new?"

Drew did his best not to growl under his throat. The pair was one of his nicer ones, a little tighter than what he usually sported at work, and he'd worn them for Will. He should have realized Jillian would comment on them.

Whipping out his hand, Drew snatched Pete's file from Jillian's hand. He had no idea why that made her laugh.

Women are so weird.

"No," Drew told her. "They're not new."

"She is right, though." Will's soft comment came from Drew's left. "Your legs do look fantastic in them."

Unable to help himself, as Drew met Will's gaze, he grinned. "Thank you, Will."

Pete snorted where he stood on his crutches to Will's left. "Did you dress up for Will?" he asked with all the candor of a teenager. "On our way home Friday, I *told* Will that you were checking out his ass." Pete snickered as he swept his gaze over Drew. "Guess you're pretty fine for an old guy."

Drew barked a laugh. "Old guy?" Leveling a mock scowl on his client, he stated, "I'll have you know, I'm only twenty-seven. That's hardly old."

"Eh." The kid didn't seem impressed — with Drew's age or his scowl. Smirking, he glanced between them. "Soooo" — he narrowed his eyes — "did you have the kahunas to really call him and set up a coffee date?"

When Will frowned at Pete, scolding him by saying his name in a warning tone, he ruined the effect by allowing his cheeks to pinken.

God, that's sexy.

Pete snickered as he glanced between them, grinning. "He did? Awesome." Lifting his fist toward Drew, he cried, "Way to go, Drew! I didn't think ya had it in ya."

"You little shit," Will grumbled, although he seemed pleased that his *little brother* appeared to like the idea of them together.

On Sunday, they'd moved from the coffee shop to a nearby diner, extending their coffee date to include lunch. There, Will had explained who Pete was to him, his *little brother* in the *Big Brother* program. While Will hadn't told him what the orphan had done to end up in the program, he'd shared that he lived in a group home in Will's school district, which had brought the young man into his orbit.

Drew thought it was damn admirable that Will would give of his time like that. He'd even mentioned it to Jake when his buddy had called him the prior evening to ask about his date. *Nosy best friend.* Jake had hummed and said he would look into it, thinking it was a really good deed.

"Wait a minute. You're a fag?"

Jillian's scandalized tone yanked Drew back to reality.

Frowning, Drew peered back at Jillian. He took in her flushed face and disbelieving expression. Her lip was curled up ever-so-slightly in a small sneer as she swept her gaze over them all.

"Wow, lady." Pete was the first to recover. "Didn't your momma teach you any manners?" He scoffed, then rolled his eyes before refocusing on Drew. "So, Drew. How do we get this started?"

Drew cleared his throat and nodded. "Let's head back to—"

"Hey, you never answered my question," Jillian cut in rudely. She even reached over her reception desk and grabbed his shirt sleeve. "I wanna know if you're a faggot?"

"Jillian, that's not appropriate behavior at the office," Alex stated, announcing his presence as he rounded the corner. "Return to your duties. We'll talk about your language later."

While Jillian released Drew's sleeve and her cheeks darkened, her eyes narrowed. "Don't you think this is something we should know?" she demanded. She even waved at Pete. "I mean, he's working with impressionable young men. What if he—"

"Do *not* finish that sentence, Jillian," Alex ordered, scowling at her. "A person's sexual orientation has no bearing on whether or not they can do the job they are hired for."

Jillian reared back as if slapped. Her eyes widened, and she shook her head. She appeared beyond shocked.

"Oh my god," Jillian gasped. "Drew *is* a faggot, and you knew!" Lifting her hand to her chest as if she were preparing to faint. "Does Mister Litman know? Surely you both can't condone his deviant behavior."

Narrowing his deep blue eyes, Alex ordered, "Jillian, I would like you to leave for the day. I'll discuss this situation with Mister Litman before contacting you this evening."

"You're sending me home?" Jillian's expression held a wealth of disbelief. "You can't be serious."

"Obviously, I am," Alex stated. "Please gather your things and go. Now."

Even as she shook her head and obeyed, Jillian mumbled under her breath about the absurdity of it all. She scowled at Drew, Will, and even Pete as she stalked to the front door. Casting one more look of disgust over her shoulder at them all, Jillian left the office.

"Well, that was dramatic, even for a Monday morning," Alex commented. He smiled blandly as he turned his attention to Pete and Will. "I'm Mister Alex Mindrid. Please call me Alex, and I offer my deepest apologies for the actions of our receptionist."

Will lifted his hand, waving away his apology. "That's not

necessary, Alex," he stated with a shake of his head. "Her actions are her own, not yours."

Alex dipped his chin in thanks. "I'll let you get on with your appointment." When he focused on Drew, his smile appeared pinched. "And I apologize to you, too, Drew. Please know her views are not shared by myself and Rafe."

Drew offered his fellow therapist a reassuring smile. "I know, Alex," he said, using his name for the first time, hoping to convey the depths of his understanding. Then Drew left Alex to what appeared to be calling in a temporary receptionist and headed toward the back. "This way, please." Drew spotted the gym bag over Will's shoulder and pointed out the locker room. "On the other side of that room, it opens into the weight room." He indicated a nearby door with the plaque *weight room* on it. "I'll meet you in there when you're ready." Giving the youngster an amused look, Drew asked, "Should I get a wheelchair for you?"

As Drew had expected, Pete rolled his eyes. "No," he grumbled before taking the bag from Will and disappearing through the doorway.

Drew turned and focused on Will. "It's nice to see you again," he murmured. He wanted to reach out and touch, but he was standing in the hallway of his work. "Are you staying or going?"

Will hesitated, then asked, "Is it okay if I watch the first couple of sessions?" He shoved his hands into his coat pockets. "That way I can help Pete or correct him with his exercises if he needs it."

"Of course," Drew assured. "Probably a good idea."

Plus, Drew loved the idea of having Will around a little while longer. He led the way into the weight room and began setting up what he needed. As they waited, Drew fidgeted with his clipboard.

After a couple of moments, Will rested his hand on Drew's

upper arm. "Are you going to get into trouble because of the receptionist?"

Drew immediately shook his head. "Naw. Don't say anythin', but she was already under review for something completely unrelated."

Will appeared relieved. "Good." He removed his hand and took off his coat. "So, would you be interested in joining me for dinner Friday night?"

Even as Drew opened his mouth, he hesitated.

Evidently, Will noticed. "Um, too soon?"

Drew quickly shook his head. "Not at all. It's just . . . I normally head to Jake and Devon's for dinner on Friday nights." Chuckling, he admitted, "Dad thinks it's date night, so he never asks me over." Drew saw the disappointment in Will's gorgeous green eyes, and he blurted out, "Will you go with me?"

Will's jaw sagged open. "Really?" He sounded as shocked as he looked. "You want me to meet your friends?"

Nodding quickly, Drew grinned. "Yeah. I do."

"O-Okay. Where? When?"

Even though Will appeared uncertain, Drew told him he would pick him up before adding his new boyfriend's address to his phone's contact information.

Excitement thrumming through him, Drew had a hell of a time focusing on his client, but he did it.

CHAPTER SIX

Excitement mixed with nerves as Drew drove to Will's house. He wondered if introducing his new boyfriend to his friends already was jumping the gun. Having never dated before, he didn't know if he was overwhelming the other man or pushing too hard or moving too fast.

I don't know anything about this shit.

Still, when Drew had told Jake that he planned to bring Will to their weekly grill night, he'd been excited. He figured if he was doing something wrong, his not-shy buddy would have told him. Hell, Jake was the one who got them together, after all.

Pulling into the driveway the GPS indicated, Drew took in the small home tucked between the trees. The neighborhood was an older one, so the home was surrounded by plenty of old-growth trees. His place had a decent-sized porch where a couple of rocking chairs were situated. As Drew climbed out of his truck, he thought it would be a nice place to enjoy a morning cup of coffee.

Drew strode up the walk and onto the porch. After a deep breath, he lifted his hand and rang the bell. Faintly, he could hear the chime ringing through the house.

In less than a minute, the door opened.

Seeing Will standing on the other side, Drew felt his breath catch. His date's dark-blue jeans fitted his body, accentuating his long, toned legs. He already had his thigh-length black coat on, but he hadn't buttoned it, allowing Drew to see the medium-green polo shirt he wore beneath.

"Damn," Drew whispered, unable to help himself. Forcing his gaze to Will's eyes, he murmured, "You look amazing."

To Drew's relief, Will's worried expression morphed into one of pleasure. He smiled and blew out a relieved breath. "I wasn't certain what the dress code would be for a weekly guys grilling gathering." Will's brows furrowed, his expression turned a little vacant, and he began mouthing a few words. A second later, Will snapped back to attention, and his smile turned sheepish. "That sounded odd, huh?"

Drew chuckled as he held out his hand. "Yeah, but cool." Wiggling his fingers, he added, "And you could have worn a pair of sweats and a t-shirt and you'd somehow have made it sexy."

Will gave him a look Drew couldn't quite interpret, but he started forward. Then he paused and grabbed something from a table in the foyer. Stepping on the porch, Will turned and locked the door behind him.

Spotting the brown paper bag with a definite cylindrical shape inside, Drew asked, "What's that?"

Holding it up, Will told him, "A gift of wine for the hosts." Drew must have had a questioning look on his face, for he added, "My mom said never go to another's house for a meal empty-handed."

Drew wrapped his arm around Will's waist, telling him, "While that's not necessary, I know Jake and Devon will appreciate it. They prefer wine over beer."

That earned him a small, relieved-looking smile from his date.

As Drew guided Will off the porch, Will asked, "Are you always this touchy-feely?"

Stiffening, Drew began to pull away. "I'm sorry. Am I being too forward?"

"No!" Will cried, easing closer to him, so Drew retightened his hold. "I like it. I just—" He sighed as he shook his head.

39

"You said you'd never dated before, so I didn't think you'd be so demonstrative."

Drew relaxed, and he grinned widely while moving Will to the passenger side of his pick-up. As he opened the door and guided his date inside, he revealed, "Well, I may not have dated, but Jake and Devon have been together for years. Another guy in our group is Devon's younger brother, Carmen, who's been with his man, Tyler, for almost a decade." As Drew leaned in and buckled Will's seatbelt, he winked at the man. "I've seen plenty of interaction between strong couples, so I know how to treat you right."

Then Drew shut the door and jogged around the front to his own side. After he'd jumped behind the wheel and fired up the engine, he pulled on his own belt. When Will hadn't responded by the time Drew had left his neighborhood, he glanced the man's way in concern.

"Everything okay?"

Will nodded. "Yeah." Chuckling softly, he added, "Never had anyone buckle my seatbelt for me before."

Drew arched one brow and asked, "Not your thing? Or should I keep doing it?"

"I . . . I'm not sure," Will admitted with another laugh. He grinned at him. "Maybe do it a few more times and I'll be able to figure it out."

"I can do that." Drew reached for the radio and turned it on. "Probably the only thing on right now is Christmas carols, but is that okay?" He pointed at his phone resting in a cup holder. "I can hook up my phone, and you can scroll through my playlists."

As the sounds of *Grandma Got Run Over by a Reindeer* filled the cab of the truck, Will laughed and waggled his brows. "Oh, you'd let me check out your playlists?" With a smirk, he claimed, "That can tell a guy a lot about someone else."

Drew snorted as he indicated his phone again. "Have at it,"

he offered even as he tried to remember if he had any songs on there that he could possibly be embarrassed about. He couldn't think of any, but that didn't mean there weren't any.

Oh, well.

As Will grabbed Drew's phone, he began to sing under his breath to the silly song on the radio.

Grinning, Drew enjoyed the sound of Will's voice. He liked it even better when Will continued to sing along to the carols, one after another. His pulse pounded oddly knowing his date felt so comfortable with him.

Drew slowed his truck and turned it into the driveway of the home shared by Jake and Devon. At that point, Will fell silent. After parking his vehicle, Drew focused on his date. He saw the flickers of uncertainty on his face and the way he nibbled his bottom lip.

What would it be like for me to nibble there?

"You okay?" Drew asked softly, doing his best to banish the thought. It had been so long since he'd kissed, and he really wanted to. Reaching over, Drew placed his hand over Will's where it was clenched on his thigh. "The guys will love you, babe."

Will snapped his attention to Drew's face. His eyebrows shot up as the corners of his lips curved a smidge. "Babe?"

Huh.

Drew hadn't even realized he'd said it. "Um." He felt his cheeks heat a little, and it was his turn to nibble his bottom lip. When Drew saw Will's focus flick to his mouth and back again, he blurted out, "I wanna kiss you, too." An idea formed. "Would that settle your nerves?"

Groaning, Will turned the hand under Drew's and gripped it. "No," he replied with a short laugh. "Walking into your friend's house with a boner from making out in your truck would definitely not make me more comfortable."

Sucking in a harsh gasp at the idea of his kiss making Will bone up, Drew dropped his gaze to the other man's groin.

Good thing there was a thick coat covering his lap. He couldn't even make out an outline of . . . anything. That didn't stop Drew's blood from heating in his veins and his dick from plumping in his jeans.

"Eyes up here, big guy," Will teased, snapping the fingers of his free hand before crooking them to urge him to lift his gaze.

Drew swallowed hard, but he did as instructed. Seeing Will's eyes twinkling, he grinned. While he was now a little uncomfortable, Drew would take it since the exchange had caused Will's unease to lessen a little.

"Come on," Drew urged. "If one of the guys spots us in the truck, we'll be ribbed for making out even when we haven't been."

Will's eyes widened a little, but he nodded and unbuckled his belt.

Once Drew had released his own clasp, he turned off the truck. He opened the door, eased out, and closed it behind him. As he moved to the front of his pick-up, he spotted Will joining him.

Drew rested his hand on the small of Will's back, wishing it was summer so he could feel the curve of his spine under his palm.

Maybe in the house.

Guiding Will up to the house, Drew told him, "Jake makes the best steaks, and Devon bakes these garlic potato wedges that are amazing. Oh, that reminds me."

Drew paused and jogged back to his truck. He opened the back door and grabbed the case of beer with one hand while sliding his other through the strap of the plastic bag. Then Drew hip-bumped the door to close it again.

"Can I carry anything?" Will asked, eyeing the items Drew carried as he returned. "Should I have brought anything else?" Then Will grimaced. "Guess I shoulda thought about that before. A food item to pass."

"Naw, don't worry about it," Drew assured. When Will remained looking dubious, he explained, "A couple only brings one dish for them both." He held up the bag a little. "Fruit salad from the store." Dipping his chin to indicate the paper-wrapped bottle of wine in Will's hand, Drew reminded, "And that wasn't really necessary. We're not pretentious around here, but I know Jake and Devon will appreciate it. They love trying new wines."

While Will didn't appear convinced, he still accompanied Drew to the door. He even opened the door when Drew instructed him to. In the foyer, Drew placed the box of beer and the bag on a bench, then toed off his sneakers.

Will followed suit with his nice shoes.

"Jake? Devon?" Drew called as he took off his coat and hung it on a wall hook. He did the same with Will's as he continued to call to his friends. "Where you at?" Having noticed Rory's car parked on the other side of the street, he added, "Ror? You here with Lester?"

They normally carpooled.

"Hey, Drew!" Lester's voice came from deeper in the house. "They just stepped out to take Jake the steaks."

"Thanks!" Drew picked up the beer. "Come on."

To Drew's pleasure, Will nodded and grabbed the plastic bag before he could. That kept his other hand free, allowing him to place it on the small of his date's back. He heard the sound of the sliding glass door moving before he made it to the kitchen.

Lester was standing in the dining room, leaning against the bar. Considering the tortilla chip that he'd just shoved into his mouth, Drew figured the man had been more interested in the pre-dinner snacks spread over the bar than going outside. Of course, since Lester avoided cold weather like the plague, that made sense.

"Hey, Drew," Lester greeted around his mouthful.

"Hey, man," Drew responded, smirking at his friend. He set his beer on the table while indicating his companion. "This is Will Hanson." Unable to help puffing up his chest, Drew added, "My boyfriend."

When Lester's gaze fell on Will, his eyes widened. He quickly grabbed a napkin and wiped his fingers. His Adam's apple bobbed as he swiftly swallowed. Finally, he held out his freshly cleaned hand.

"Hi, Will," Lester greeted as they shook. "Great to meet you. Drew told us a little about you"—his gaze cut to Drew for a second before refocusing on Will—"just last week." After releasing Will's hand, Lester smirked as he waggled his eyebrows. "Boyfriend already, huh? You guys must work fast."

Drew growled softly while seeing Will's cheeks take on a light pinkish hue. "Don't make me knock the shit out of you, Lester," he growled.

Lester laughed as he brought his bottle of beer to his lips. "I—"

"Have a bad sense of humor," Rory cut in, slapping Lester upside the head as he passed him, causing him to swallow beer the wrong way and begin hacking. Then he stuck out his hand. "I'm Rory Meantz. This idiot's ride for the night."

Will took Rory's hand. "Nice to meet you."

"Hey, I'm Jake," the man greeted, waving from the kitchen where he was cleaning up the tray that must have held the marinating steaks. "Glad to have you here." He pointed at the bar. "Help yourself to whatever. We just put the steaks on, so it'll be about fifteen. Oh, how do you like yours cooked?"

"Uh, medium-rare, if that's okay," Will replied.

Jake gave him a thumbs up, then returned to cleaning.

"And I'm Devon, Jake's husband," Devon stated, stepping forward with his hand out. "Welcome to our home. It's nice to meet you."

Will shook once more, then held out the bottle of wine. "Thank you for having me."

Devon took it, and his black eyebrows lifted as he read the label. "Oh, this is a good one." He grinned at Will. "Excellent taste. Shall I open it for you?"

"Uh, I actually brought it for you," Will told him.

Nodding and heading toward the kitchen, Devon stated, "Then I'll join you for a glass." He showed the bottle to Jake. "What do you think?"

Jake turned and pinned Will with a wide grin. "You are very, *very* welcome here." Then he laughed and winked.

Drew grinned upon hearing Will's answering chuckle, knowing his boyfriend would fit right in.

CHAPTER SEVEN

W ill found he was having a fantastic time. He'd never considered himself very confident or comfortable in new groups, but he had to admit, Drew's friends were a great bunch of guys. They did their best to make him feel welcome, from asking about him to teasing him just like they did everyone else.

While eating dinner, Will was surprised to discover that he recognized Jake. "Hey, you went to college with us, right?" Watching Jake chew while nodding, Will had another epiphany. "You were roommates." The memory of that long-ago kiss flashed through his mind as well as the words the jocks had exchanged. "And you were on the football team."

Jake grinned after he swallowed. "My freshmen year, yeah," he confirmed. "Decided it wasn't my thing, so I quit before my second year."

After that, the standard conversations ensued. He learned who did what for a living as well as their hobbies and interests. When Will shared that he knew how to play half a dozen instruments, Lester's jaw sagged open.

"Wowee!" Lester cried, putting down his knife and leaning closer. "I can't imagine how long that must have taken. Your dedication must be impressive!"

Will shrugged, uncomfortable with the praise. "It just sort of happened," he admitted. "I learned drums first. I played a snare drum for a couple of years in high school and was in the marching band," Will revealed, trying to explain. "I can't do a thing with stringed instruments, but wind instruments, flutes, trumpets, and trombone styles, things you have to blow into, after the first couple, I picked up the rest easy."

Drew reached over and gripped his wrist, squeezing lightly. "That's amazing, babe."

Chuckling, Will met his gaze. "There's that babe again. Is that what you're going with?" he teased. In truth, Will liked it. He'd never had a boyfriend give him a pet name before.

Before a slightly blushing Drew could respond, the sound of a door opening echoed from the front of the house. A second later, a deep voice called, "Sorry we're late, Jake! Tyler's meeting ran later than expected."

"It's okay, Carmen," Jake called back, leaning away from the table and peering toward the hallway that led to the front door. "I put your steaks in the oven to keep warm. Everything else is spread out on the counters. Grab plates and join us."

Devon frowned. "Funny how my brother apologizes to you and not me," he grumbled.

Jake snickered as he winked at his husband. "That's because *I* cook him an epic steak just the way he likes it."

Will had to admit as he took another bite of his meat, Jake was indeed a grill master.

A man similar in size and build to Devon's thick African American frame appeared. On his arm was a slender, geeky-looking redhead with glasses and freckles. They were introduced as Devon's younger brother, Carmen, and the man's significant other, Tyler. After greeting Will, they made up their plates and joined them.

They'd just finished the meal and were heading toward the front living room with fresh drinks when Drew's phone rang. He pulled it out. When he read the screen, he frowned but accepted the call.

"Hey, Dad," Drew greeted. "Is everything okay?" Under his breath, he whispered to Will, "He hasn't called me on a Friday night in years."

Will nodded. When he glanced around, he saw everyone was currently focused on Drew. Evidently, a phone call from Dad got everyone's attention.

"Yeah, Dad. I'm on a date," Drew said into the phone. At the same time, he wrapped the arm holding his beer around Will's waist, pulling him closer. "It's our second one, although we've talked and texted on the phone for a while now. I'm hopeful."

While they *had* talked every evening on the phone and shared numerous texts throughout the week, Will thought calling it *a while* might be stretching it. Still, he knew he seemed to be clicking with Drew super fast. He'd never meshed with any boyfriend so swiftly.

And isn't calling us boyfriends a little quick, too?

Huh. Oh, well.

Will liked it.

"Her name?" Drew asked, his words refocusing Will's attention to the fact that the man was talking to his father.

Will watched Drew close his eyes, reopen them, then glance around at his friends. Following his gaze, he saw a mixture of expressions varying from encouraging to pensive to understanding. Then Drew focused on Will, meeting his gaze.

Drew licked his lips before smiling at Will. "Not a *her*, Dad. His name is Will Hanson, and I knew him in college. We recently ran across each other again, and the spark never died." He said all that while staring at him. Whatever his father said caused Drew to narrow his eyes. "Dad, you know that's bullshit. Being gay isn't something that rubs off on you. I just told you there was a spark in college." Drew growled softly into the line, then stated, "No, Dad. I'm sorry I never told you I was gay, but it's the reason I didn't want to pursue professional ball. I didn't want to spend my life hiding. I like the life I've built."

Listening to Drew's one-sided conversation caused Will's

gut to churn. While the man had said he would tell his father the truth, he sure hadn't thought it would be after one week. He hoped meeting him again wouldn't ruin Drew's relationship with his father.

Shit. Is this my fault?

Will attempted to pull away, but Drew furrowed his brows and shook his head. He even tried to tighten his hold on him, although the beer in his hand made it difficult. Will stilled anyway, not wanting to upset his already frustrated . . . boyfriend.

"Look, Dad. I'm sorry this came as a shock, and I know I shouldn't have done this over the phone," Drew began, his tone taking on a placating note. "But you always told me that all you ever wanted for me in life was for me to be happy. How about I come over on Sunday? It's Christmas Eve, so I wanted to see you anyway, and we can talk about how happy Will makes me." After another second, Drew sighed and nodded. "Yeah. Thanks, Dad. I'll see you then."

When Drew hung up his phone and slid the device onto the holder attached to his belt, he grinned broadly as he swept his gaze over his friends. "Well, that went better than I expected, actually."

Lester stared at him wide-eyed. "You just came out to your dad . . . *over the phone.*"

Drew nodded. "I did. I didn't want Will to think I was embarrassed about being with him." He guided Will the rest of the way into the living room. When Drew urged him onto a sofa and sat next to him, he sighed deeply. "After all, nothing could be further from the truth."

"Um, so what did he actually say?" Rory asked curiously from where he perched on the other end of the sofa.

Devon had settled on a large chair and had pulled Jake onto his lap. Carmen and Tyler had sprawled on a second sofa, and Lester relaxed in another chair. Good thing the living space was so large.

49

"You know the age-old drivel," Drew replied with a roll of his eyes. "I'm confused because I hang out with you guys so much. But I've always been so athletic and played football so well. Are you sure you just haven't met the right woman?"

Will felt a little bad, since he'd heard some of his own friends' parents say such things. Women had asked him stuff like that, too. It seemed to take so long to convince some people that being gay wasn't a choice. As the song said, we're born this way.

"So, you're going to visit with him on Sunday?" Devon commented. "Do you need back-up?"

Drew shook his head. "Naw. My dad will understand eventually." While grimacing, he added, "Although it'll probably be awkward for a while. You know how it is."

Devon chuckled. "Yeah, I do, although when I came out, it was easy because my brothers had done it first."

Carmen scoffed. "*I'm* the one who took the edge off our pops. I think Brendan damn near gave him a heart attack." When Will glanced between the brothers uncertainly, Carmen grinned. "Brendan is our eldest brother, almost like a second father, really, after our mom left us." He smiled fondly though, so probably thinking of his brother, not his mom. "I had lunch with my dad and had just come out to him because I didn't want Tyler to be a dirty little secret anymore." Turning his head, Carmen pecked Tyler's temple. "You didn't deserve that."

"I wasn't really a secret, per se," Tyler murmured back softly. "But I sure appreciated it."

After another kiss between the clearly loving couple, this one on their lips, Carmen returned his attention to Will. "Anyway, after lunch, we tried to reach Brendan, but it kept going to voicemail. We figured he was doing something for his coaching job, so we, uh, drove to his condo. We planned to let ourselves in, since we knew where he hid a key, and wait for him." For some reason, perhaps from the tone of his voice, Will guessed that if Carmen didn't have dark-chocolate skin, he would have been blushing. "Anyway, we walked in and, uh . . . Brendan was home with his boyfriend, and they were . . . kissing."

"Kissing?" Will didn't think that sounded so bad.

While Carmen nodded and grimaced, Tyler snickered. "I wasn't there, but I was told about the definite tongue-action, passion, and clothes that needed to be adjusted before they were presentable." He blinked innocently as he added, "Carmen says it scarred him for life."

"I did not say that," Carmen countered, scowling at his man.

Tyler lifted one shoulder in a half-shrug. "Not in so many words, maybe."

Devon chuckled. "Hence, our father and the near heart attack."

"Is your father okay? Did he handle it eventually? Did he yell or something?" The questions tumbled from Will's mouth, and he couldn't seem to stop them. "He didn't disown all of you, did he?"

"Our father is fine," Devon assured with a smile. "He asked the traditional, *was there something I did wrong* question, the *are your sure* question, and there was the *maybe you just haven't met the right woman* comment, but after a couple glasses of alcohol and some time, he accepted it just fine."

Carmen butted in with, "It helps that Brendan gave him the grandson he's been dying for, giving Nick an out for a while."

Devon nodded sagely. "True. True."

"Oh, did your brother adopt?" Will asked curiously. "Since I've always known I was gay, I've looked into it."

"You've looked into it?" Drew questioned. "When? Why?" He shook his head sharply. "Okay, not why. I can answer that.

Hell, you're a role model to foster kids in the *Big Brother* program. Of course you'd want to raise kids of your own."

Seeing the tension lines around Drew's eyes, Will realized they might have just discovered something they didn't agree on. "Uh. Do you not want kids?"

Drew took in a long, slow breath, his wide torso expanding. "I'm not saying that," he replied slowly, clearly choosing his words carefully. Holding his gaze steady, Drew admitted, "Just that, I've never taken a partner before, so it never even ended up a blip on my radar." He used the neck of his beer bottle to point around the group. "None of us have kids, so I've never been around them. I guess I never really thought about it."

"Oh. Okay." Will figured he should be honest. "I'm looking into adopting Pete."

Drew stared at him in shock, and his lips parted in surprise. "O-Okay," he whispered, blinking quickly. "I-I'll need time to process this, but please know I'm not averse to, um, raising a kid."

Will couldn't help but chuckle at Drew's flabbergasted expression. "Drew, Pete wouldn't be thinking of me as a parent," he assured, patting his leg. "We'd think of ourselves more as brothers. He's already fourteen, remember?"

As Will watched, Drew blew out a clearly relieved breath.

"Right." He grinned. "Okay. A brother I could handle."

As everyone in the room laughed, joshing Drew about his responses, Will realized he was fixated on something else Drew had said.

Partner? Is Drew really thinking that long-term already?

CHAPTER EIGHT

With how quiet Will was when Drew drove him home, he figured the events at the barbcque were both good and bad. Good—his buddies had made his man feel more than welcome. Bad—his dad had ended up calling at the most inopportune time.

Drew had kept his promise, to be honest with his father, and Will had seemed beyond surprised.

"So, do you mind if I ask a question?" Drew decided to address that.

Will stopped humming along with *Sleigh Ride* which was playing on the radio and turned his head to focus on him. "Ask anything, but I reserve the right to not answer."

Nodding, Drew accepted that. "Okay. A request then. If you don't want to answer, tell me that." He reached over and squeezed Will's thigh. "I want only honesty between us in our relationship."

"You know, we've only known each other a week," Will pointed out. "Yet, you use terms like boyfriend, relationship, and partner. Isn't that moving too fast?"

Sure, it felt like warp speed, but he didn't mind.

Drew shrugged. "I guess I'm just trying to be honest and straightforward about where I see us going," he admitted with another squeeze to Will's hand. "Anyway."

"Right." Will nodded. "Your question."

"Why were you surprised that I told my father the truth on the phone?" Drew glanced Will's way before returning his focus to the dark, wet road. When he didn't get an answer right away, he flicked his gaze to Will again while saying, "I told you I intended to share the truth with him. That the only reason I hadn't was because I'd never found someone worth coming out to him for. I never intended to lie to my father should I find someone I wanted to spend the rest of my life with."

After a few seconds where the only sound was the tires on wet asphalt, Will replied, "I'll answer honestly if I get to ask the next question."

"Fair enough," Drew replied. "Anything."

Will nodded. "Okay. So, my first two years of teaching, I dated a guy in the closet. He kept telling me, over and over, that he was going to come out to his friends, family, and colleagues. I believed him, even though every time he introduced me as a co-worker."

"He taught at the same school as you?" Seeing Will nod, Drew couldn't help but ask, "Does he still?"

Chuckling, Will murmured, "I thought I got to ask the next question."

Drew grimaced. "Sorry."

"It's okay," Will countered, squeezing his hand in return. "Was just joking. Um, no, he doesn't still work there, thank god." Scoffing, Will finished, "I figure he's still in the closet and probably cheating on his wife of three years now . . . assuming they're still together."

"H-He dumped you for some, uh—" Drew couldn't fathom walking away from Will, and he hadn't even managed to taste his lips again. "Naw." Drew decided differently. "You dumped *his* ass, right?"

Boy was I tempted to taste his lips so many damn times tonight, and I'm not walking away from his door without giving it my best shot at kissing him goodnight.

Will hummed as he nodded. "Yeah, I did end up dumping him. After that, he tried to get me fired a couple of times, but as it turned out, I had more friends at the school than he did."

Drew noticed Will turning his head to focus on him from the corner of his eye as he commented, "Evidently, a few of the staff knew about us but never said anything. After all, I was openly out. When he started slandering me, he ended up getting in trouble for discrimination."

Drew laughed as he grinned at the road. "Nice."

"Anyway, he switched to a different school and found some poor girl to trap into marriage," Will told him. "So I was surprised that you were so honest with your father, since we've only been on a couple of dates."

"Okay." Drew understood. "Just so you know, I always follow through with what I say I'm going to do." Glancing Will's way again, he added, "Of course, if I do need to break a commitment, I'm equally upfront about that, too."

Will smiled. "I like that."

Grinning, Drew asked, "Okay. So . . . your question?"

After a second of hesitation, Will asked, "You said that you hadn't bothered to tell your father because you'd never found someone who made you think about having a relationship."

Drew arched one eyebrow. "There isn't a question in there."

"Well, how can you think, after only a week, that *I* could be that person?" Will squeezed his hand as he hurried to add, "Not that I'm not flattered, but, well, how? Why?"

Humming, Drew took a second to give that question the consideration it was due. "Well," he began slowly, choosing his words carefully. "I already told you that your kiss is the one I held all others against and they never measured up, so I know our chemistry will be explosive."

"So this is all physical?" Will asked, sounding disappointed.

Drew shook his head. "I'm not done answering," he told him, bringing their twined fingers to his lips and kissing Will's knuckles lightly.

He'd seen Devon do it to Jake often, and it always brought a smile to his buddy's lips. To his pleasure, as a street lamp illuminated Will's face, he saw a similarly sweet smile on his date's lips. There was some surprise, too, but that was okay.

I'll get him used to my touch.

"I wouldn't come out to my dad for something just physical," Drew told Will, continuing his explanation. "I've gotten physical release easily over the years." He figured he ought to be upfront that he wasn't a virgin by any means. "You've crossed my mind on more than one occasion."

Spotting Will's driveway, Drew paused and pulled his hand away. He parked, then turned his attention to his date — the man he wanted to continue to explore a future with. Reaching over, Drew again took Will's hand.

"Although we never really knew each other, Will, I've never forgotten you," Drew admitted as he took in Will's lean handsome features. "And now that we're getting to know each other, everything I learn about you makes me more attracted to you, and I don't mean physically. Your work in the *Big Brother* program shows me your kind and compassionate heart. Your ability to learn so many instruments denotes your hard work ethic." The moonlight coming in through the window allowed Drew to see the way Will's cheeks were darkening, and he couldn't resist bringing his free hand up to skim his forefingers along one with the backs of his fingers. "Then there's the way you respect yourself, shown when you refused to be in a secret relationship. Also, your thoughtfulness in bringing a gift to Jake and Devon even though I told you it wasn't necessary. Your —"

Will lifted his hand and placed it over Drew's lips. "Stop," he whispered huskily. Awe filled his expression as he eyed him, his head shaking just a smidge. "We've only been chatting for a week, and you came to all those conclusions?"

Drew smiled against Will's fingers, enjoying the feel of the other man's hands on him. "I know jocks have a reputation for being self-centered and, well, dumb." He winked, letting Will know he didn't necessarily think he felt that way. "So I learned to keep my mouth shut most of the time. That made me get better at observing stuff. I see a lot more than most would think, considering my size."

"Lots of assumptions made," Will whispered as he skimmed his fingers away from Drew's lips and along his jaw. "Same with band geeks."

"And the color of women's hair," Drew whispered absently. The hairs on his nape stood on end at the feel of Will's fingers skimming along his jaw, and it was becoming difficult to think. "Or computer nerds."

"I want to ask you in for a drink," Will murmured, holding his gaze. "But I don't really want a drink." His expression turned heavy-lidded as he slid his focus to Drew's lap, then back to his eyes. "Unless it's a certain liquid."

There was no misinterpreting Will's look, and a groan slipped from Drew's lips, unable to be kept in. His cock throbbed behind his fly, suddenly hard as steel and leaking. Drew's breath caught in his chest, and goose bumps erupted on his arms.

"Do you think that's too forward of me?" Will whispered.

Drew's mind was shutting down with the strength of the arousal surging through him, making it difficult for him to process Will's words. It took him a few seconds to realize the man had asked a question. It wasn't until Will pulled his hand from Drew's face that he recognized that he needed to respond. After all, he really wanted to remove the pensive look on Will's face.

"Not too forward, at all," Drew claimed, his body nearly burning up from the inside out. "Especially since if I get my hands on your body, I'm going to be too forward right along with you and demand you allow me to hold you all night long."

Will groaned softly as he nodded eagerly. "Yes, please."

That was enough for Drew. He pulled away from Will and turned off his truck. After unbuckling his belt, he exited and shut the door behind him. Drew glanced toward the passenger side and saw Will had done the same.

Drew hurried forward, meeting Will halfway up the walk. As he watched his soon-to-be lover pull out his keys, he pressed close to his back, invading his space. Resting his hands on Will's hips, he dipped his head and nuzzled his lips along the side of his neck.

To Drew's satisfaction, a satisfying shudder worked through the man he held. He wanted to explore that response so very much. Drew wondered what else would cause shivers, shakes, and trembles.

"Y-You're making it difficult to o-open the door," Will told him, his voice husky and low.

Drew continued to slide his lips along Will's neck as he replied, "I'd say I'm sorry, but that would be a lie." Then, after a nip on the lobe of his ear, he lifted his head. "But I want to get you into the house, so—" Drew lowered his hands, but he didn't move away from him.

Will moaned softly, the noise going straight to Drew's already stiff dick. His blood thrummed in his veins, causing his fingers to twitch. He desperately wanted to take the man into his arms again and peel the coat from him.

As soon as Will opened the door and led the way inside, Drew did just that. He slammed the door closed and locked it, then grabbed Will. After swiftly unbuttoning the nice coat, Drew pushed it off Will's shoulders.

To Drew's pleasure, Will wasn't a passive party. He had immediately unzipped Drew's coat. In order to remove them, they had to release each other, which they did at the same time.

Two heavy thumps sounded in the foyer as their coats hit

the floor.

Unable to resist the man in front of him a second longer, as soon as his arms were free, Drew grabbed Will. The other man wrapped him up in an equally frenzied hold, rubbing over his fabric-covered back. Drew dipped his head and captured his new lover's lips. With a nip on his bottom lip, Drew demanded entrance.

Will gave it, opening immediately to him.

Drew pushed his tongue into Will's mouth, sweeping in to taste the other man. As he enjoyed the flavor of wine and the food they'd eaten that evening, he discovered something else, something that had to be all Will. The sweet tang caused his taste buds to sing, and Drew knew he would never get enough.

As Drew continued to map Will's mouth, exploring and plundering, he pushed his hands under the other man's polo shirt. Upon feeling the smooth flesh of his man's back, he groaned into his new lover's mouth. He clutched him close as he rubbed up and down his spine, stopping one hand at the waist of the jeans that had caused his ass to look fantastic all evening.

Dipping one finger under the fabric, Drew slid it into Will's crack and teased the sensitive flesh.

In response, Will moaned and yanked out of the kiss. His cheeks were flushed, and his lips were beautifully wet and swollen. He peered up at him through glazed eyes.

"Bedroom," Will demanded. "Now."

"Hell yeah," Drew replied, more than on board with that.

CHAPTER NINE

Will couldn't remember the last time he allowed his dick to do the thinking. Everything about Drew turned him on. From his touches to his attitude to his speech, everything about him lit Will up from the inside out.

Having reached the bedroom, Will turned and faced Drew. The man's brown eyes had darkened nearly to black. His gaze smoldered as he reached for the hem of Will's shirt.

Obeying the silent command, Will lifted his arms and allowed Drew to pull it from his body. He instantly returned the favor and removed Drew's shirt. The jeans, socks, and shoes disappeared in short order.

Then Will found himself lifted and placed in the middle of his bed. He stared at Drew in shock upon experiencing his easy strength. The big man panted, but something told Will that it was from lust, not exertion.

Maybe it was the massive rod jutting from Drew's groin, the tip already damp from pre-cum. His thick erection was just as stunning as the rest of the man. Drew sported thickly muscled limbs and an eight-pack.

Will had never seen one of those in person. He normally didn't feel self-conscious about his body. After all, he ran and was normally careful about what he ate, keeping himself in shape. Compared to Drew, though, Will felt downright skinny.

"God, you're so fucking sexy, Will."

Drew's growled words yanked Will's attention to his face. The man stood beside the bed, staring down at him with fierce hunger etched on his features. The lust Drew felt practically burned in his eyes.

"You're the sexy one," Will replied, his voice huskier than he'd ever heard it before. "You've got a fricken eight-pack."

With a roll of one boulder of a shoulder, Drew dismissed his comment. "Condoms? Lube?"

Will pointed at the nightstand on the other side of the bed. Then, before Drew could round the bed, he rolled onto his hands and knees. Leaning over, he opened the drawer and pulled out the requested items.

As Will drew back, he felt the bed dip to his left. A low growl filled the room, the sound one of appreciation, and he peered over his shoulder. He spotted the feral hunger etched over Drew's features right before the man rested his hands on Will's back, right above his ass cheeks.

"So fucking stunning," Drew rumbled as he slid his hands down and palmed Will's globes. He squeezed and massaged Will's flesh as he gently prized his cheeks apart. "Oh, damn, Will. You have a beautiful tan hole." Sliding a thumb into Will's trench, Drew teased it over his striated opening. "Can't wait to feel this wrapped around my cock." His voice held a definite whining note to it. "It'll feel so good."

Will clenched his hole on reflex, having seen the steel pipe jutting from between Drew's legs. His erection was perfectly proportioned to his body — thick, long, and veiny. The man's massive rod had to be at least nine inches.

"Relax," Drew crooned, massaging his entrance some more. He'd obviously felt Will stiffen. "I'll have you good and relaxed, babe. Don't you worry."

Before Will could tell Drew that he was clenching in anticipation, not concern, Drew moved his hands to his hips and flipped him back over. Will would forever deny his squeak of surprise, but he knew Drew had heard him from the flicker of amusement lighting his dark eyes.

Drew held out his hand, and Will gave him the condom.

Arching one brow, Drew quickly opened it. As he rolled it down his length, Drew stated absently, "I've never fucked bare before, but I look forward to it." He grinned as he met Will's gaze. "When you're comfortable with me, we'll get tested." Reaching down, Drew gripped Will's erection and began jacking him slowly. "Lookin' forward to feeling this in me, your hot cum warming up my insides."

Will hissed, his stomach muscles clenching and releasing. Sparks erupted through his groin at the stimulation on his dick. It took Will a second to process Drew's words.

"Y-You'd let me—" Will gasped as Drew massaged his frenulum while skimming a nail along his piss slit. "Drew!"

It had been far too long since he'd felt the touch of another's hand, and his body felt primed. His balls began to tingle as he clenched his abs, trying to control himself. He groaned as he twisted his fingers into the comforter while watching Drew play with his erection.

"St-Stop," Will whined. "Too close."

Drew's husky chuckle sounded dark and rough. "Well, we wouldn't want that to go to waste," he commented with a wink.

Then Drew bent, opened his mouth, and swallowed Will's cock to the root.

Wet, sucking heat enveloped Will's sensitive flesh. The pressure coupled with the view of Drew between his legs, servicing him, went straight to his head. Tensing, Will barked a cry as he bucked.

Drew clamped a hand onto Will's hip, stilling his action. Tipping his head a little, he peered up at him through his lashes. He even leered while still continuing to suck him strongly, his expression one of hunger.

Will's gut clenched at the lascivious look, and when Drew's other hand rubbed over his hip, a shudder worked through his body.

Drew began bobbing on his dick, slow and steady. Each time he lodged Will's cock head in his throat, he swallowed, massaging his cap. As he sucked strongly and pulled upward, he replaced his lips with his hand and squeezed his wet shaft. The hand on his hip shifted position, fingers teasing into his groin hairs, tickling the sensitive flesh beneath while still holding him in place.

The mix of squeeze and massage, heat and pull, yanked Will to the edge so swiftly, he almost didn't have time to warn Drew. He gasped his lover's name, but he didn't pull off. Instead, Drew moved his hand to Will's balls and gently squeezed his orbs.

Roaring with bliss as fiery zings coursed through his veins, Will cried out his pleasure. He arched his back as shudder after shudder racked his body. Blissful endorphins caused spots to dance across his vision, and he felt as if he were floating.

Will wasn't certain how long he drifted, reveling in the aftershocks of the endorphins pinging through him. His senses reeled, and his whole body trembled. Zings shot through him, and his skin goose bumped.

Coming back to himself at the sensation, Will realized his dick remained mostly hard. Drew continued to suckle him lightly, stimulating him. In fact, that wasn't the only thing stimulating him.

Will peeled open eyelids he couldn't remember closing and looked down his body.

Drew met his gaze and smiled around his mouthful of meat.

Gasping, Will clamped down on the two fingers in his chute. Then Drew pegged his prostate, sending a fresh zing of pleasure through his groin. Still holding Will's gaze, Drew slid his other hand up Will's body and gently gripped his nipple.

Sparks shot across his chest, and both nipples beaded in response.

"Drew," Will whimpered, desperately needing to move. "Please."

Popping off Will's dick, Drew lifted his torso. He wiped his mouth with the back of his hand, then placed that one next to his shoulder as he levered over him. All the while, Drew continued to finger Will's channel.

"You're so beautiful in your passion," Drew growled, leaning over him. "Love this flush on your skin, seeing your nipples beaded, and the sweat of arousal glistening on your skin."

Will groaned as he untangled his fingers from the comforter. "God, the things you say," he mumbled as he pulled him close. "Fuck me already."

Then Will lifted his head and captured Drew's lips. He reveled in the way the bigger man fed him a growl. A second later, Drew threaded his fingers into Will's hair and tugged, forcing him to turn his head.

Drew deepened the kiss, and Will hung on for the ride as his dominant lover ravished him. He pressed their torsos together, the skin sliding deliciously. His fingers played with his ass, the pinch and burn telling Will that Drew fitted another finger inside him nearly instantly disappeared.

Will rode those fingers with abandon, causing his cock head to rub against Drew's ripped abdominals. His blood fired through his veins, burning him anew. He clung to Drew, relishing the way the other man fucked his tongue into his mouth, imitating what would come next.

Just when Will thought he would need to beg, Drew's fingers eased from his chute. He whined into the bigger man's mouth, but then he felt the bump of something blunt at his entrance. Will felt the push, the stretch, and he moaned at the bite of pain.

Separating their lips, Drew turned his head and placed his lips against his ear. "Push out, Will," he urged. "I need inside you so fucking badly."

Needing the exact same thing, Will did as he'd been instructed. He pushed out as he let out a long breath. His body gave way and accepted the massive intrusion that was Drew's erection.

Drew groaned roughly as he sank a little way into Will before pausing. His warm breath teased over the shell of his ear, causing the hairs on his nape to stand on end. Shivers of pleasure trickled down his spine.

"More," Will urged, rocking against Drew's body. He tightened and relaxed his chute muscles, doing his best to entice him. "Give me more." He put the bite of an order into his tone. "I want all of you, Drew."

"P-Promised not to hurt you." Drew's voice sounded ragged and thick, betraying how he barely maintained control.

"You won't," Will reassured, rubbing down Drew's sweaty back and feeling his straining muscles. "You're not."

Then Will lifted his legs and wrapped them around Drew's thighs. At the same time, he gripped the man's rock-hard ass. Using his hold, Will rocked up as he tugged Drew's body to him.

Drew roared in obvious bliss as Will forced his erection deep into his body. The thick rod filled him to capacity, and Will moaned in pleasure. Never had he felt so full, and his heart thudded in his chest with the exquisite sensation.

"Will," Drew hissed as he froze, his heavy body pinning Will to the bed. Lifting his head, he peered at Will, his eyes holding a mixture of burning lust and concern. "You okay?"

Grinning at Drew, Will sighed. "Oh, yeah. More than." Skimming his palms back up to Drew's broad shoulders while keeping his legs around him, he ordered, "Fuck me, Drew."

Drew growled as his eyes narrowed. "The things that come

out of your mouth."

Then Drew obeyed. He eased partway out before slamming back into him. His powerful body picked up speed, plowing into Will over and over.

With each stroke, Drew slid across Will's prostate, sending his senses soaring, the man's every move seeming to propel him to the pinnacles of ecstasy.

Sooner than Will thought possible after exploding from the best blowjob ever, Will felt his balls pull tight once more. His eyes rolled back in his head, and his orgasm slammed into him. Calling Drew's name, he rode the waves of his release.

Vaguely, Will heard Drew's answering roar. As their bodies stilled, their skin damp with sweat, he felt his lover petting his side while keeping his weight off him a smidge with his other. Sighing with satiation, Will pressed kisses along Drew's jaw.

"You ruined me for anyone else," Will whispered before he could catch himself.

Drew lifted his head, a loopy grin curving his lips. "Good."

CHAPTER TEN

Drew had just experienced the best thirty-six hours of his life. He'd spent Friday night with Will in his arms. They'd spent Saturday together, lounging around his boyfriend's house, mostly in the buff. Drew couldn't count the number of times they'd had sex, and his ass was deliciously sore.

Between bouts, they'd talked, sharing all sorts of things about each other. He'd never talked with any of his one-night stands before, having no interest in learning anything about them. That was how Drew knew Will was *the one*. He wanted to know *everything* about him, even trivial stuff, like how he preferred the toilet paper to be loaded on the reel.

When Drew had asked to see Will after getting together with his father on Christmas Eve, his lover had asked about Christmas traditions. He'd told them that since it had just been him and his father, they'd rarely done much for the holiday. After Drew had left home, they did little more than exchange a phone call on the actual day and gifts on whichever day they saw each other near the date.

"A phone call? Really?" Will had sounded incredulous. "How is that even possible?"

"When you meet him, you'll understand," Drew had told him. "He doesn't celebrate any holiday. I normally spend Christmas with Jake and his family. Do you want to come?"

"I spend it with my mom," Will replied.

"Why don't you both come?" Drew had countered. He really wanted to see his man every day. "And can I see you after

I talk to my dad tomorrow?"

"My band is marching in the evening Christmas Eve parade in town," Will told him. "I don't know what time we'll wrap it up."

"That's awesome!" Drew grinned. "I'll be there." Waggling his brows, he stated, "I can't wait to see you in your uniform. Can I peel it off you when you get done?"

Will tipped his head back and laughed. "I normally change before heading home, but I suppose I could make an exception." Then he sobered and told him, "I'll talk to my mom. She's probably already got the menu half prepped, but maybe she'd like a change." Cocking his head, Will asked, "You sure Jake and his family won't mind?"

"Naw." Drew shook his head. "They believe in the more, the merrier."

On his way home, Drew had immediately called Jake. He'd confirmed what he'd told Will, and if they decided to join them, he and his mother would be welcome. His buddy then began teasing and or grilling him about his Saturday, talking to him the whole way home.

Drew pulled into his driveway and frowned, taking in his garage door. His hand hovered over the button attached to his truck's visor for a couple of heartbeats before he lowered it to the wheel. Shaking his head, Drew wondered who would do such a thing . . . and on Christmas Eve.

"Drew? Is everything okay?" Jake's voice came through the line.

"Actually, no," Drew replied. "Um, does your dad have any jurisdiction in our area?"

Jake's father was a detective, but he lived several towns over almost two hours away.

"Noooo," Jake replied, drawing out the word. "What's wrong?"

Drew sighed, shaking his head. "Someone graffitied my garage door with a rather unflattering message."

"A gay slur?" Jake guessed, his voice hardening.

"Yeah."

Jake growled under his breath. "Hang on. I have Detective Haralson's number. Let me give it to you."

"That the guy who handled the break-in at your place a few years ago?" Drew asked for confirmation.

"Yup."

"Why do you still have his number?" Drew asked curiously as he drummed his fingers on the wheel. "That was several years ago."

"He's on my Christmas card list."

Drew chuckled. Only his friend. About a week before Christmas a few years prior, a burglar had been looting homes. He'd broken into Jake's home and had been stopped by a goose that was pegged for their Christmas supper. The animal was their pet now.

"I just sent you his contact card," Jake told Drew right before his phone dinged, indicating a text message.

"Thanks, man."

"You got it. Call me and update me later."

Drew agreed, then hung up.

Ten minutes later, Drew had explained to the detective who he was, how he'd gotten his number, and why he was calling. Detective Haralson agreed to be there as quickly as possible, which would be another ten minutes.

Sitting in his truck, Drew waited. He put his seat back and called his dad. "Hey, Dad."

"Hello, son," his father greeted. "Since you're supposed to be here in an hour and you're calling me, I assume there's a problem?"

At least he's still talking to me.

"Afraid so." Drew explained.

"I'll be there shortly."

Without another word, Drew's father hung up.

Drew was about to close his eyes and doze—he hadn't gotten a whole lot of sleep over the last two nights—when a tap came on his window. Turning, he spotted Mrs. Nettle from across the street. She'd always been nice to Drew, baking him cookies and other items he'd had to work hard to burn off. In return, he took out her garbage, mowed her lawn, and shoveled her walk.

As Drew lowered his window, he wondered if discovering that he was gay would change her behavior toward him.

Only one way to find out.

"Hi, Mrs. Nettle," Drew greeted with a smile. "Happy Christmas Eve."

"Always so polite." Mrs. Nettle smiled back at him. "Happy Christmas Eve to you, too."

Spotting his father's vehicle approaching, Drew asked, "Is there something I can do for you, ma'am?" He glanced toward her house. "Do you need your walk salted?"

Mrs. Nettle shook her head. "No, dear. I'm actually here to help you." She held up a rather expensive-looking digital camera. "Have you called the cops, yet? I have pictures of who did that to your garage." As Drew sat there gaping at the elderly woman, she continued, "It was done less than an hour ago, and I was debating on calling them myself or not." Scowling, Mrs. Nettle stated, "I'm so sorry. I should have called as soon as I saw her spraying the garage door. After all, who paints at this time of year? I guess I was just too shocked. Then her body obscured some of the writing, and it wasn't until she was almost done that I figured out what the words said." She shook her head. "Such disgusting behavior—"

For a second, Drew thought she was referring to gays, since that was what the message was about. Fortunately, her continued ranting eased his concerns.

"—as if who a person loves is anyone's business but their

70

own." Then she smiled brightly at him and patted his hand where he was resting it on the window's ledge. "Do you have a nice young man to spend your holidays with?"

Drew couldn't help but grin. "Yes, I do. I'm going to see him later today."

"Oh, how lovely," Mrs. Nettle replied.

By then, Drew's father had joined him as had another man. The stranger was tall and slender with deeply bronzed skin. He wore an open jacket despite the chilly weather, revealing the butt of his service weapon in a shoulder holster.

Drew began opening his truck's door, and Mrs. Nettle obligingly moved out of the way. "Are you Detective Haralson?" he asked as he stepped out of the vehicle.

"I am. Are you Drew Menard?" the man asked.

"Yes, sir." Drew held out his hand. "Thank you for coming." After they shook, the detective peered at the slur and arched one brow, so Drew turned his attention to his father and murmured, "Thanks for coming, Dad."

His father clapped him on the shoulder and nodded. "Of course, son." He glanced from him to Mrs. Nettle before refocusing on Drew. "So, you're seeing your young man tonight? Uh, Will, you said, right?"

Drew nodded, trying to gauge his father's reaction through his expression. "I am. He's the drum major for the Colina High School, and he's leading the marching band in the Christmas Eve parade tonight."

Mrs. Nettle clapped her hands. "Oh, my goodness. I'm going to that." She bounced on her toes as if she were a young girl. "I can't wait to see him." With a wink and while lowering her voice in a conspiratorial manner, she stated, "Men in uniform are so sexy, aren't they?"

While talking about what he found sexy in front of his father made him feel distinctly uncomfortable, he refused to leave the older lady hanging. Especially since she was being so supportive. He dipped a nod and very solemnly replied, "Yes, ma'am."

"Oh, poo." Mrs. Nettle popped him on the arm. "Don't you ma'am me." Then she turned and focused on Detective Haralson, who was taking pictures of the damage. "Now, Detective. I have evidence for you."

After that, Drew really didn't have to do much other than admit that he did indeed know the person in the pictures—Jillian Parsons—and explain why she might hold a grudge—losing her job for discrimination at the office.

Detective Haralson told him that he would have her picked up and charged.

To Drew's surprise, his father asked to join him at the parade. He couldn't remember the last time he'd done anything holiday-related—any holiday—with his father. Too shocked, he just nodded.

That evening, Drew stood beside his dad watching the parade. They'd chatted a little at Drew's place. As it had turned out, his father was more upset that Drew had never told him the truth. Of course, giving him the day to calm down had helped, or so his father had claimed.

"I hear a band," his father claimed, peering up the street. "The drum major is in front, right? Or is he playing a drum?"

"Out front, although he started by playing the drums," Drew replied. He'd ended up looking it up on his phone during the prior week. "He should be easily recognizable because he'll be carrying a baton and have a fancier uniform."

His father hummed.

"Hey, Drew. Hey, Mister Menard," Jake called, announcing his arrival. "We made it just in time!"

Drew grinned as he fist-bumped his friend. "Yep. Looks like it."

"Jake," his father greeted him with a handshake. "Good to

see you again, son."

As his father greeted the others in the group—everyone had managed to find them just in time—Drew turned his attention back to the parade. He spotted his man immediately and sucked in an appreciative breath. His heart felt as if it skipped a beat as lust pooled in his belly and heated his blood.

Will looked stunning in his blue and red uniform coat with gold accents, red dress slacks pressed to perfection, and matching red cap. Shiny black shoes, white gloves, and a black baton completed his outfit. He marched in front, his movements precise and sure, each foot barely leaving the ground since the parade was moving at a snail's pace.

That was okay with Drew because it meant he could ogle Will all he wanted.

"Well, well, well," his father murmured beside him. "So that's him, huh?"

Drew glanced at his father, who had his focus down the street, having obviously spotted Will. Nodding, Drew murmured, "Yeah. That's my man."

His father patted him on the shoulder. "Good-lookin' guy, son. And a teacher, you said. Impressive."

Grinning, Drew just nodded again.

As Will drew near, Drew's friends whooped and hollered, drawing attention to themselves. Will flicked his gaze their way, never missing a beat. A slight smile curved his lips.

Through a series of commands and a blow of a whistle, Will started the band on a rousing version of *Sleigh Ride*.

No wonder my man hummed along to it in the truck.

Drew watched with pride as Will and his band continued down the path. The music filled the street—cymbals clashing, instruments playing, and drums pounding—making his ears ring. Some in the crowd sang along with the carol, and Drew and his friends—and to his surprise, even his father—joined in.

As Will and his band disappeared around a corner, Drew

turned to check out the rest of the parade. He knew he would see his lover before too long. Will had told him he would return to where he was on the parade route after finishing, and Drew planned to be waiting right there until he came.

While waiting, Drew realized his life had changed swiftly in just over a week—he'd come out to his father and had been accepted, the woman harassing him at work had been removed from his life, and he'd found the love of his life.

Thanks be to a little holiday magic.

Frogs Legs and Goose Feathers
Charlie Richards

Excerpt

Jake Lewis bobbed his head as he sang along with the Christmas carol. Leaning forward in his driver's seat, he squinted through the windshield. The darkness and heavy snowfall made seeing too far in front of him tough.

"Fiiiiiive golden rings!" Jake felt the wheels of his Jeep slide a little and snapped his mouth shut. Gritting his teeth, he white-knuckled the steering wheel. When Jake felt the tires catch on the freshly fallen snow, he relaxed back into his seat and started singing along again—under his breath, however, since most of his concentration was still on the road and getting home safely.

" . . . seventh day of Christmas my—shit, it's a snowstorm, moron. Slow down," Jake snapped as he saw a car slide through the four-way stop intersection in front of him. Shaking his head, he waited and watched the driver re-gain control and trundle off. Jake started across the intersection. " . . . to me, seven swans a-swimming, six geese a-laying, fiiiiive . . ."

Jake turned into the driveway of the home he shared with

his partner, Devon Gateman. After hitting the button to open the garage door, he smiled. Seeing Devon's BMW already inside, he knew his big, dark-skinned lover had beat him home.

As Jake parked, he found he wasn't surprised. Devon worked less than fifteen minutes from their home as a chiropractor who owned his own practice. That meant he could set his hours and change them if need be . . . like when a snowstorm blew in.

Jake was in his senior year of college and wasn't nearly as fortunate. Snow or not, his afternoon class had still been held. Since Jake was working to get top marks for his Bachelor of Science degree, he couldn't skip his advanced biology class.

After turning off his Jeep, Jake grabbed the strap of his school satchel. He opened his door and slid from the vehicle. As Jake closed the door, he slung the bag over his shoulder. Jingling the keys in his right hand, he hurried to the door, a spring in his step.

Not only couldn't he wait to see Devon — even after almost three years, his love for the amazing man still seemed to be growing — but he loved the holidays. They were planning to trim the Christmas tree that evening. As Jake opened the man-sized garage door that led into the laundry room, he could already hear the carols filling the house.

Jake grinned, enjoying the soothing tones of Elvis Presley singing about being blue for Christmas. Shaking his head, he chuckled under his breath. Learning Devon had a secret infatuation with The King had been a surprise, but since Jake enjoyed most of his music, he didn't mind.

After toeing off his sneakers, Jake removed his coat, hat, and gloves, hanging them up to dry. He hummed along with the song as he exited the room and entered the kitchen. Setting his bag on the counter, he rummaged through it until he found the plastic container that had held his lunch sandwich. That he opened, rinsed in the sink, then placed into the dishwasher. After rinsing the plastic baggy he'd used for his dill spear, he placed it upside-down in the drain rack to dry.

Jake glanced around, surprised to see that Devon hadn't appeared, yet. "Devon?" he called, picking up his bag and heading through the dining room and toward the stairs.

He'd just placed his foot on the first step when he heard Devon holler back, "That you, Jake?"

But that wasn't why Jake had paused. Cocking his head, he stared at the baby gate spread across the open French doors that led to Devon's home office. Scratching his head, Jake set his satchel on the steps, then headed that way.

Reaching the blocked off room, Jake couldn't help the way his jaw sagged open in shock. His lover's desk had been pushed to one side, and all the books that had been on the bottom three shelves had been piled upon it. There were newspapers spread out on the floor as well as a kiddie pool in the corner. Towels curved around the exterior of the plastic, water-filled item, probably to offer extra stability as well as to soak up spilled water.

However, Jake's gaze remained riveted on the animal placidly eating from a doggie-style bowl full of what appeared to be spinach and lettuce.

"Devon?" Jake shouted, confusion mixing with alarm. "Why is there a goose in your office?"

God, what a weird thing to ask.

Jake heard Devon's slow, slightly awkward gait as his lover descended the stairs. His man had been in a car accident years before they'd met, and his knee and thigh were heavily scarred. While it limited Devon's mobility at times, Jake never found the man lacking in any way.

Still, Jake couldn't seem to pull his attention away from the goose. When he'd hollered, the animal's head had jerked up. It began honking and heading toward Jake, so he backed up a few steps.

He didn't know how long a goose's reach was, or if it was strong enough to get through the gate. Hell, for all Jake knew it could fly over the barrier. After all, it was a bird.

"Hi, hon," Devon greeted, wrapping his arms around Jake

from behind. He dipped his head and nuzzled Jake's neck with his soft goatee hair. "Welcome home."

Jake tipped his head to the side, giving Devon more room. Resting his hands over his dark-skinned lover's strong forearms, he hummed appreciatively. As much as he loved the feel of Devon's facial hair teasing along his neck, even that couldn't distract Jake.

"Hi, Devon. Thanks." Then Jake returned to his original inquiry. "Why is there a goose in your office?"

Devon chuckled, the sound deep and husky in a way that caused Jake's balls to tingle and his blood to flow south.

Damn, my man does it for me.

"Well, I want to cook a nice goose dinner for you, your fathers, and my family, but I couldn't find it at any of the local stores," Devon told him, his voice low, almost wary as he whispered the words into Jake's ear. "When I looked online, all the reputable sites were already sold out or wouldn't get it here by the twenty-third."

"So . . . you bought a live one from somewhere?" Jake knew he sounded incredulous, but he couldn't help it.

Devon rubbed his hands up and down Jake's stomach. "Yeah. I found a place an hour north that had a couple left and drove up there after work." Teasing his lips along the sensitive bit of flesh beneath Jake's ear, he crooned, "We only have to keep it in here for a couple of days. I'd originally planned to keep it outside, but then the snowstorm rolled in." Hugging Jake tight to his chest, Devon purred, "Please don't be mad, baby."

Jake groaned as he sagged in Devon's embrace. As odd as finding a goose in Devon's office was, he couldn't gather any ire. His amazing man was just too sweet for words, trying to plan something special.

"Not upset," Jake assured as he turned in Devon's hold. He lifted his arms and wound them around his lover's neck. Rocking his hips, Jake offered stimulus to his quickly hardening dick. Meeting Devon's concern-filled, deep-brown eyes,

Jake smiled at his man. "Just a little unexpected."

Devon's expression betrayed his relief. "Thanks, Jake."

Without waiting for another word, Devon tightened his arms, dipped his head, and sealed his lips over Jake's.

ABOUT THE AUTHOR

Charlie started writing fantasy when she was eight, and after stumbling onto her first erotic romance at age nineteen, she realized her true calling. She now focuses on writing gay erotic romance, normally of the paranormal variety, with heroes of all kinds. With the help and support of her husband, Charlie finally fulfilled one of her life-long goals . . . move to acreage with her horses. You can often find her curled up with her laptop and a cup of tea or glass of wine, creating her next adventure. Charlie enjoys exploring the mountains of her new Oregon home on horseback, 4-wheeler, or motorcycle.

She can be reached at ch.richards2010@yahoo.com
Or visit her at www.charlie-richards.com

www.ingramcontent.com/pod-product-compliance
Lightning Source LLC
Chambersburg PA
CBHW070535130626
46555CB00003B/1434